I SURVIVED

THE SINKING OF THE *TITANIC*, 1912

I SURVIVED

I SURVIVED

THE SINKING OF THE *TITANIC*, 1912

by Lauren Tarshis

illustrated by Scott Dawson

Scholastic Inc.

NEW YORK   TORONTO   LONDON   AUCKLAND
SYDNEY   MEXICO CITY   NEW DELHI   HONG KONG

Text copyright © 2010 by Dreyfuss Tarshis Media Inc.
Illustrations copyright © 2010 by Scholastic Inc.

This book is being published simultaneously in hardcover by Scholastic Press.

ISBN 978-1-338-84582-2

10 9 8 7 6 5 4 3 2 1   22 23 24 25 26

Printed in the U.S.A.   40
This edition first printing, April 2022
Designed by Yaffa Jaskoll

FOR DAVID

ACKNOWLEDGMENTS

I'd like to thank my agent, Gail Hochman, for all she did to bring this series to life. I am also grateful to my wonderful editor at Scholastic, Amanda Maciel, and to Ellie Berger and Debra Dorfman, for welcoming me to the world of Scholastic books. Ben Kanter and Aaron Leopold helped me get this right. And to my children, Leo, Jeremy, Dylan, and Valerie, who make every day a thrilling journey.

The statistics and facts in this book were drawn mainly from two sources: *A Night to Remember*, by Walter Lord (Henry Holt, 1955) and *Titanic: The Ship Magnificent*, Volumes I and II, by Bruce Beveridge, Scott Andrews, Steve Hall, and Daniel Kistorner (The History Press Ltd., 2008).

CHAPTER 1

MONDAY, APRIL 15, 1912

2:00 A.M.

ON THE DECK OF RMS *TITANIC*

The *Titanic* was sinking.

The gigantic ship had hit an iceberg.

Land was far, far away.

Ten-year-old George Calder stood on the deck.

He shivered because the night was freezing cold.

And because he was scared. More scared than he'd ever been before.

More scared than when Papa swore he'd send George to the army school, far from everything and everyone.

More scared, even, than the time the black panther chased him through the woods back home in Millerstown, New York.

The deck of the *Titanic* was packed with people. Some were running and shouting.

"Help us!"

"Take my baby!"

"Jump!"

Some just plain screamed. Children cried. A gunshot exploded across the deck. But George didn't move.

Just hold on, he told himself, gripping the rail. Like maybe he could hold up the ship.

He couldn't look down at that black water. He kept his eyes on the sky. He had never seen so many stars. Papa said that Mama watched over him from heaven.

Could Mama see him now?

The ship lurched.

"We're going down!" a man shouted.

George closed his eyes, praying this was all a dream.

Even more terrible sounds filled the air. Glass shattering. Furniture crashing. More screams and cries. A bellowing sound, like a giant beast was dying a terrible death. George tried to hold the rail. But he lost his grip. He tumbled, smashing his head on the deck.

And then George couldn't see anything.

Even the stars above him seemed to go black.

CHAPTER 2

19 HOURS EARLIER...
SUNDAY, APRIL 14, 1912
7:15 A.M.
FIRST CLASS SUITE, B DECK, RMS *TITANIC*

George woke up early that morning, half expecting to hear Papa calling him for chores.

But then he remembered: the *Titanic*!

He was on the greatest ship in the world.

It was their fifth day at sea. George and his

4

eight-year-old sister, Phoebe, had spent two months in England with their aunt Daisy. What a time they had! As a surprise for George's tenth birthday, Aunt Daisy took them to see the Tower of London, where they used to chop off your head if the king didn't like you.

Now they were heading back to America.

Back to Papa and their little farm in upstate New York.

George got out of bed and knelt by the small, round window that looked out on the ocean.

"Morning," said Phoebe, peering through the silk curtains of her bed and fumbling for her spectacles. Her curly brown hair was practically standing straight up. "What were you looking for?"

George had to smile. Phoebe always had a question, even at the crack of dawn.

Maybe that's why she was the smartest little sister in the world.

"I thought I saw a giant squid," George said. "And it's coming to get us!"

George rushed over and grabbed Phoebe with wiggly squid arms. She curled up into a ball and laughed.

She was still laughing when Aunt Daisy came in. Even in her robe and slippers, Aunt Daisy was the prettiest lady on the whole ship. Sometimes George couldn't believe she was so old: twenty-two!

"What's this?" Aunt Daisy said. "You know the rule: No having fun without me!"

Phoebe sat up and put her arms around George. "Georgie said he saw a giant squid."

Aunt Daisy laughed. "I wouldn't doubt it. Everyone wants to get a look at the *Titanic*. Even sea monsters."

George halfway believed it. He'd never imagined anything like the *Titanic*.

Aunt Daisy called the ship a floating palace. But it was way better than the cold and dusty castles they'd seen in England. They had three whole rooms — one for Phoebe and George, one for Aunt Daisy, and one for sitting around and doing nothing. They even had a man, a steward named Henry. He had bright red hair and an Irish accent that made everything he said sound like a jolly song.

"Some fresh towels for your bath?" he would say. "Some cocoa before bed?"

And just before they turned out the lights for the night, Henry would knock on their door and peep his head in.

"Is there anything else you might need?" he'd ask.

George kept trying to think of *something* he needed.

But what could you ever need on the *Titanic*?

The ship had everything, even a swimming pool with ocean water heated up like a bath, even gold silk curtains for your bed so you could pretend you were sleeping in a pirate's den, even three dining rooms where you could eat anything you wanted. Last night George had eaten two plates of roast beef, veal and ham pie, carrots sweet as candy, and a mysterious dessert called meringue pudding. It tasted like sugary clouds.

Actually, there *was* one thing missing from the *Titanic*: the New York Giants baseball team. George wondered what Henry would say if George said, "I need shortstop Artie Fletcher right away!"

Probably Henry would say, "Coming right up, sir!"

George grinned just thinking about it.

But Aunt Daisy wasn't smiling at him. She looked very serious.

"We have to make the most of our last three days at sea," Aunt Daisy said in a low voice. "I want you to promise me, George. *No more* trouble!"

George gulped.

Was she really still mad at him for last night?

He'd slid down the banister of the grand staircase in the first class lobby. How could he

resist? The wood was so shiny and polished, curving around like a ride at the fair.

"That lady could have moved out of the way," George said.

"How could she?" Phoebe said. "She was wearing a hundred pounds of diamonds!"

Aunt Daisy almost smiled. George could tell.

No, she could never stay mad at George for long.

Aunt Daisy put her face very close to George's. She had freckles on her nose, just like George and Phoebe.

"No more trouble," she repeated, tapping his chest. "I don't want to have to send a telegram to your father."

George's stomach tightened into a baseball.

"Don't tell Papa!" Phoebe said. "He'll send George away to that army school!"

"I'll be good," George promised. "I will, really."

"You better be," Aunt Daisy said.

CHAPTER 3

George didn't mean to get into trouble.

It's just that he got these *great* ideas.

Like on their first day at sea, when he had climbed up the huge ladder into the crow's nest.

"Aunt Daisy!" he'd yelled, waving his arms.

She had looked up. And she'd almost fainted.

And yesterday George had explored the entire ship. Aunt Daisy kept warning him that he'd get lost. She said the ship was like a maze. But George could always find his way. Even in the huge forest that stretched out behind their farm. Mama used to say that George had a map of the world behind his eyes.

He saw the engine rooms and the boiler rooms, and wound up on the third-class recreation deck. He was watching some boys play marbles when he noticed that he wasn't alone. A little boy was staring up at him with huge eyes the color of amber glass.

"See," the boy said. "See."

And he held out a postcard of the Statue of Liberty. He looked so proud, like he'd carved that big lady himself. George felt like he had to show something in return, so he took out his good-luck charm, the bowie knife Papa had given him for his ninth birthday. He let the little boy run his fingers across the handle, which was carved from an elk's antler.

"Enzo," the little boy said, puffing out his chest and pointing to himself.

"George," said George.

"Giorgio!" the little boy cried with a smile.

A man sitting near them laughed. He was reading an Italian-English dictionary and had the same huge eyes as the boy. George guessed right that he was Enzo's father.

"Marco," he said, shaking George's hand. "You are our first American friend."

Marco must have been studying that dictionary pretty hard, because George understood everything he said. George learned that Enzo was four years old. He'd lost his mama too. He and Marco came from a little town in Italy, and now they were moving to New York City. George told Marco about their farm and their trip and explained that any decent person living in New York had to be a Giants fan. For some reason, Marco thought that was funny.

When it was time for George to leave, Enzo got upset. Very upset.

"Giorgio!" he howled, loud enough for the entire ship to hear.

People stared and put their hands over their ears. Marco promised that they'd see George again, but Enzo wouldn't quit howling. George had never heard anything so loud.

By the time Enzo let go of George's leg and George ran back up to the suite, Aunt Daisy was practically howling too.

"I thought you fell overboard!" she cried.

But even then she wasn't really mad.

She didn't get *really* mad until last night.

How that lady screamed when George came sliding down the banister — like he really was a giant squid.

George didn't mind getting yelled at. He was used to it. Not a day at school went by without Mr. Landers shouting "George! Settle down!" And Papa, well, he always seemed to be mad at George.

But not Aunt Daisy. And being on this trip was supposed to make her happy, happy for the first time since her husband died last year. It had been Uncle Cliff's dream to be on the maiden voyage of the *Titanic*. He'd struck it rich selling automobiles and had plenty of money to pay for one of the biggest suites on the ship.

When Uncle Cliff had his accident, George was sure Aunt Daisy would cancel the trip. Instead she'd invited George and Phoebe to go with her.

And to George's shock, Papa said they could.

"Your aunt's going on this trip to find a little peace," he'd said to George. "I expect you to be a perfect gentleman."

And if he wasn't, George knew he'd be shipped off to that army school for sure. Papa had been talking about that place ever since George had brought the two-foot rat snake to school to show Mr. Landers—because they were studying reptiles!

George had been perfect the whole time in England. He'd let Aunt Daisy drag him to a fancy clothes store for a new pair of boots. He even learned to drink tea without spitting it back into the cup.

But, well, the *Titanic*.

The ship gave him so many great ideas!

But now he'd really be perfect.

No more ideas for the rest of the voyage.

CHAPTER 4

Phoebe wasn't taking any chances with George.

"I'm not letting you out of my sight," she announced after they'd finished breakfast. "I'm your guardian angel."

"I didn't know angels wore spectacles," he said, tugging on one of Phoebe's curls.

"The smart ones do," Phoebe said, grabbing George's arm. She offered him a lemon drop from the little silver tin she'd been carrying around since London.

George made a face. He hated those old-lady candies.

George wanted to go find Marco and Enzo and hear more about Italy. He wanted to ride the elevators up and down. Hardly any other ship in the world had elevators! Better yet, he wanted to find Mr. Andrews, the ship's designer.

When Mr. Andrews had stopped by their table at dinner the first night, George thought he was just another boring millionaire coming over to kiss Aunt Daisy's hand.

But Mr. Andrews was different.

"You *built* the *Titanic*?" said George.

Mr. Andrews smiled. "Not by myself. It took thousands of men to build her. But I did design her, that's true."

He invited George and Phoebe to come with him to the first class writing room. He unrolled the ship's blueprints across a long, polished table.

It was like looking at the skeleton of a giant beast.

"She's the biggest moving object ever built," Mr. Andrews explained. "Eleven stories tall. Forty-five thousand tons of steel. And longer than four city blocks."

"Our aunt says nothing bad can happen to this ship," Phoebe said. "People say it's unsinkable."

"No ship is safer," Mr. Andrews said. "That is certainly true."

"What if the *Titanic* was hit by a meteor?" said Phoebe, whose latest obsession was outer space. She was determined to see a shooting star before they docked in New York.

Mr. Andrews didn't laugh or roll his eyes like Mr. Landers did when Phoebe asked her questions.

"I hadn't planned on any meteors hitting the ship," Mr. Andrews said thoughtfully. "But I'd like to think she could take almost anything and still float."

Phoebe seemed satisfied.

"Are there any secret passages?" said George.

Mr. Andrews studied his blueprints, and then pointed to the boiler rooms.

"There are escape ladders," he said. "They run up the starboard side of the ship, up two decks, through the stokers' quarters, and into their dining hall. I hear the crew likes using them instead of the stairs."

George could have stayed there all night. He

asked a million questions and Mr. Andrews answered every single one.

"I was like you when I was a boy," Mr. Andrews said just before Aunt Daisy came to haul George off to bed. "One day I predict you'll build a ship of your own."

George knew that would never happen. He could barely get through a day at school. But he liked that Mr. Andrews said it. And he sure wanted to find those secret ladders.

But Phoebe had different ideas.

First she dragged George to the first class library so she could check out a book on Halley's comet. Then she took him on a walk on the boat deck. He felt like a dog.

"Strange," Phoebe said, looking at the lifeboats that hung just off the deck. "There are only sixteen boats. That's not nearly enough for everyone."

"The ship's unsinkable," George said. "So do we really need lifeboats at all?"

Phoebe stared at the boats and shrugged. "I guess you're right," she said. And then she announced that it was time to see how many ladies were wearing hats with blue feathers.

George groaned.

This would be the most boring day of his life.

But at least nobody was yelling at him.

CHAPTER 5

At dinner that night, Aunt Daisy raised her glass. "To George! No trouble for one entire day!"

They clinked their glasses together just as an old man stopped by their table.

"Mrs. Key," the man said to Aunt Daisy. "I've been meaning to say hello."

"Mr. Stead!" Aunt Daisy said. "What a pleasure. This is George, my nephew, and Phoebe, my niece."

Mr. Stead nodded hello.

"So," Aunt Daisy said. "What brings you onto this magnificent ship?"

"Oh, I couldn't miss it," he said. "I think all of society is on this ship. I hear there's even an Egyptian princess on board."

"Really!" Aunt Daisy said. "I haven't met her!"

"Well, none of us have. She's traveling in the first class baggage room."

"Excuse me?" Aunt Daisy said.

"The princess is more than twenty-five hundred years old," Mr. Stead said.

George's ears perked up.

"I'm not sure I understand," Aunt Daisy said.

"She's a mummy," Mr. Stead said.

"A mummy!" Phoebe gasped.

"That's right," Mr. Stead said. "From a tomb near Thebes. I understand she belongs to a man named Mr. Burrows. People are saying he sold the coffin to the British Museum. Then he packed the princess herself in a wooden crate. Apparently he's bringing her back for his collection. Some say it's bad luck to take a mummy from its tomb."

"I'm glad I'm not the superstitious type!" Aunt Daisy said.

Mr. Stead chuckled. "In any case, nothing can harm this ship. Not even the curse of a mummy!"

Mr. Stead tipped his hat and said good-bye.

"Mr. Stead is a very famous writer in England," Aunt Daisy said. "You never know who you'll meet on the *Titanic*!"

And then it hit George, the best idea ever.

That mummy! He had to see it.

Maybe this day wasn't so boring after all.

CHAPTER 6

George didn't tell Phoebe or Aunt Daisy about his plan.

He figured he'd head down to the first class baggage room after they went to sleep. He'd find Mr. Burrows's crate, pry it open, and take a quick peek at the mummy. He'd be back in bed and snoring away before anyone knew he was gone.

It was almost eleven-fifteen when Phoebe was

finally asleep and the light was out under Aunt Daisy's door. George crept out of bed. He quickly got dressed and put his knife in his pocket. He'd need it for prying off the lid of the crate. And who knew? Maybe there was a live cobra in the box too. George could hope, couldn't he?

George opened the door and peeked into the hallway. He wanted to avoid Henry, who seemed to have eyes in the back of his bright orange head. He wouldn't like George creeping around so late at night.

But the hallway was quiet. There was no noise at all except for the quiet hum of the engines, rising up from the bottom of the ship. George loved that noise. It made him think of crickets in the woods at night.

In fact, being out here all by himself reminded him of the nights at home when he sneaked out into the woods while Papa and Phoebe were asleep.

He'd head out when his mind was filled with restless thoughts.

About why Papa was always mad at him, or why he didn't try harder in school.

And of course Mama.

Almost three years had passed since she died. George tried not to think about her too much. But some nights when he closed his eyes, he'd remember her smile. Or her smell when she hugged him close. Like fresh grass and sweet flowers.

And that song she'd sing to wake George up in the morning:

> *"Awake, awake.*
> *It's now daybreak!*
> *But don't forget your dreams. . . ."*

Thinking about Mama was like standing close to a fire. Warm at first. But get too close and it hurt too much.

Much better to stay clear of those thoughts.

Nothing cleared George's mind quicker than being in the woods. He never stayed out for more than an hour or two. . . . Except for that night back in October.

George was heading back toward home when he heard a terrible sound, like a little girl screaming. He turned around, and in the dark distance he saw two glowing yellow eyes.

Some old-timers said there were black panthers in the woods, but George never believed it.

But as the yellow eyes got closer, George could see the outline of a huge cat, with two glistening fangs.

George told himself not to run. He knew he'd never outrun the panther.

But he couldn't help it—he ran as fast as he could. Branches cut his face, but he didn't slow down.

Any second the panther would leap up and tackle George. Its claws would tear him apart.

George could feel the cat right behind him; he could smell its breath, like rotting meat. George grabbed a fallen branch. He turned and waved it in front of him. The panther lunged and grabbed the branch in its jaws.

George let go of the stick and scrambled up a tree, climbing as high as he could go.

The cat dropped the branch and came after him, like a shadow with glowing eyes.

George pulled out his knife.

He waited until the cat's front paws were on the small branch just below him. And then, with all his might, he chopped at the branch with his knife.

Crack.

The branch broke free.

The giant cat tumbled through the air, screaming and crashing through the branches, and then hit the ground with a thud.

There was silence.

And then the cat stood up. It looked up at George for a long moment.

And it turned and walked slowly back into the woods.

George stayed in the tree until it was just about light, and made it into bed just before Papa woke up.

His friends at school refused to believe George when he told them, even when he swore on his heart.

"No way."

"Big fat lie."

"Next thing you'll be saying is that you've been signed by the Giants." Their laughter rose up around George, but it didn't bother him, because right then he realized that it didn't matter what they thought.

George knew he'd faced down the panther.

And he'd never forget it.

CHAPTER 7

Just thinking about seeing the mummy made
George happy. He went down five flights of stairs
to G deck and practically skipped along the long
hallway toward the front of the ship. He ducked
into doorways a few times to hide from the night
stewards. But he had no trouble finding his way,
not like Phoebe, who got lost walking from the
dining room to the washroom.

"Next time I'll leave a trail of bread crumbs,

like Hansel and Gretel," she'd said, their first day on board.

"How about lemon drops?" George had suggested.

Phoebe had giggled.

The hold was in the very front of the ship, past the mail sorting room and the cabins where the stokers and firemen stayed. Too bad, George thought, that there wasn't time to sneak in and see the escape ladders. Luckily there were two more days at sea.

George walked right through the doors of the first class baggage room and down a steep metal staircase that led to the hold. All around him were crates and trunks and bags neatly stacked on shelves and lined up on the floor.

It took him a minute to figure out that everything was arranged in alphabetical order, by the owners' names, and a few minutes to find the *B*s.

And there it was, a plain wooden crate stamped with the words:

MR. DAVID BURROWS
NEW YORK CITY
CONTENTS FRAGILE

George smiled to himself.

This was going to be easy.

He took out his knife and started to pry off the lid. He worked carefully, prying each nail loose so he'd be able to close the crate tight again when he was finished.

He'd made it halfway around when he heard a strange sound.

The hair on his arms prickled.

It was the same feeling he'd had the night of the panther, that someone — or something — was watching him.

George stared at the crate, his heart pounding.

And before he could even take a breath,
something leaped out of the shadows and pushed
him to the ground.

George looked up, half expecting to see a
mummy rising out of the crate, her arms reaching
for George's throat.

What he saw was almost as horrifying.

It was a man with glittering blue eyes and a scar running down the side of his face.

He grabbed George's knife out of his hand. The man was small, but very strong.

"I'll take this," he said, admiring it. Then he looked George up and down.

"So," the man said. "Trying to fill your pockets with some first class loot?"

George realized he must be a robber. George had caught him in the act!

"Uh, no, I'm . . ."

The man pointed to George's boots. "Which trunk did you steal those from? Cost more than a third class ticket, I'd say."

George shook his head. "I got them in London," he said, and too late realized he'd made a mistake.

"Ah, a prince from first class," the man said with a hearty laugh. "Just down here for a little thrill? What's your name?"

"George," said George softly.

"Prince George," the man said, bowing in a joking way. "A pity those boots wouldn't fit me," he added, standing up. "But you do have something I'd like. Your key. Always wanted to see one of those first class cabins."

There was no way George could let this man up to the suite! He'd jump overboard before he let him near Aunt Daisy and Phoebe.

"There's a mummy down here!" he blurted out. "It's worth millions! It's in that crate!"

The man raised an eyebrow.

George kept talking.

"I thought I could sneak it off the ship and sell it in New York," George lied. "My father's business is bad. I thought if I could sell it . . ."

The man looked at the crate.

"I like the way you think," he said.

He waved the knife at George and told him not to move. And then he quickly worked the knife around the lid. Obviously he'd done this many times before.

He lifted the lid off the crate. But before either of them could look inside, there was a tremendous rumbling noise, and the entire hold began to shake so hard that George almost fell. The shaking got stronger and stronger, the noise louder and louder, like thunder exploding all around them. A trunk tumbled off a shelf and hit the scar-faced man on the head. The knife clattered to the floor, but George didn't try to get it. Here was his chance to escape. He spun around, ran up the stairs, and darted out the door.

CHAPTER 8

George ran as fast as he could down the hall. He heard shouting behind him, but he didn't stop until he was back on B deck, safe again in first class.

A steward hurried past him with a stack of clean towels.

"Good evening, sir," he said.

George nodded, out of breath.

Nothing could happen to him up here, he knew. So why was his heart still pounding?

It was the ship, he realized — that thundering noise. That shaking in the hold. Had a boiler exploded? Had a steam pipe burst?

An eerie silence surrounded him, and George's heart skipped a beat as he realized that the engines had been turned off. The quiet rumbling had stopped.

Just outside, George heard people talking loudly. Did they know what was happening?

George went out onto the deck and walked over to the small crowd of men. Most were still dressed in their dinner tuxedos and puffing on cigars. They were standing at the rail, pointing and laughing at something happening on the well deck, one level below. What was so funny?

George squeezed between two men and looked over the rail.

At first he was sure his eyes were playing tricks. It looked like the well deck had been through a winter storm. It was covered with ice and slush. A bunch of young men in tattered coats and hats were pelting each other with balls of ice, roaring with laughter like kids having a snowball fight.

"What's happened?" asked a man who'd walked up behind George.

"The ship nudged an iceberg!" said an old man with a bushy mustache. He didn't sound worried.

An iceberg!

"Is that why they've stopped the engines?" said the new man. "Because of some ice on the deck?"

"Just being cautious, it seems, following regulations," said the older fellow. "I spoke to one of the officers. He assured me we'll be underway any moment. Hey there!" he yelled down to the young men below. "Toss some of that ice up here!"

One of the gang picked up a piece of ice the size of a baseball. He threw it, but the man with the bushy mustache missed. George reached out and made a clean catch with one hand. The crowd cheered. George held up the ice and smiled. Then he held it out to the man.

"Keep it, son!" he said. "There's plenty for everyone."

The piece of ice was heavier than George had expected.

He sniffed it and wrinkled his nose.

It smelled like old sardines!

More ice balls came sailing up from below, and the men jostled to catch them.

Their laughter and cheers rose up around George, and the fear he'd felt in the baggage hold faded away. From up here, on the deck of this incredible ship, George felt powerful. Nothing could hurt him on the *Titanic*.

Not a meteor falling from space. Not a giant squid.

Not the scar-faced man.

George squinted out into the distance, hoping to see the iceberg, but the sea faded into darkness.

His teeth were chattering now. It was so much colder than it had been at dinnertime. He wanted to be back in bed, curled up under his fancy first class sheets and blankets.

The corridor was still quiet as George crept toward his suite.

As he was letting himself in, he stepped on something that made a crunching sound under his boot. At first George thought that it was ice or a piece of glass. But when he picked up his heel, he saw that the carpet was covered with yellow crystals.

George smiled. It was just one of Phoebe's lemon drops.

George let himself in, easing the door shut.

Phoebe's bed curtains were closed. The light under Aunt Daisy's door was off.

George quickly changed into his pajamas and climbed into bed.

Yes, he was safe, he told himself.

He tried to go to sleep, but as the minutes ticked by, his mind got restless.

It hit him that his knife was gone, forever,

and the total silence of the ship seemed to press down on him. Why hadn't the engines started up again?

He lay wide awake, listening and wondering.

It was almost a relief when he heard someone knocking on their door.

CHAPTER 9

It was Henry.

"Hello, George," said Henry. "Can I speak to Mrs. Key, please?"

Henry wore his usual polite smile, but his voice wasn't jolly.

"What is it?" said Aunt Daisy, stepping out of her room.

"So sorry to barge in like this, ma'am," Henry said. "But there's been an . . . incident."

Aunt Daisy glared at George.

"I'm so sorry, Henry," she said in an exasperated voice. "My nephew here just can't seem to stay out of trouble!"

"Oh, no, ma'am!" Henry exclaimed. "This has nothing to do with George. It's the ship, ma'am. Seems we've bumped an iceberg. I'm sure the captain is just being cautious, but he wants everyone up on deck."

"It's after midnight," Aunt Daisy said with a laugh. "Surely the captain doesn't expect us to appear on deck in our nightclothes!"

"No, ma'am. It's very cold outside." Henry walked over to the dresser and brought out three life jackets. "And you'll need to put these on. Over your coats."

Aunt Daisy stared at the life jackets as if Henry was holding up clown costumes.

"Henry! I'm not taking the children out into the cold for some kind of drill! Has Captain Smith lost his senses?"

"Of course not, Mrs. Key," Henry said. "Now

if you could get yourself and the children ready. I'll be back in just a moment to see if you need any help."

He left them alone.

"All right, George," Aunt Daisy said. "I guess we'll have another adventure to boast about when we get back. You get dressed. I'll get Phoebe up."

Aunt Daisy went to Phoebe's bed, pulling aside the curtains.

George heard a gasp, and he rushed over.

Phoebe wasn't there.

"Where could she be?" Aunt Daisy exclaimed.

A cold feeling crept up George's spine. Phoebe, his guardian angel. She must have woken up while George was gone, and now she was somewhere on the ship. Searching for George.

He took a deep breath.

"I went out exploring," George said. "After you

went to bed. I didn't think Phoebe would wake up. She never does!"

"So she's out there looking for you?" Aunt Daisy said.

George nodded. "She doesn't want me getting into trouble." He kept his eyes glued to the floor. Aunt Daisy should be furious with him, and Papa was right! George had no sense. Not one lick of sense.

How would they ever find Phoebe?

But then George had an idea . . . that lemon drop in the hallway.

Could it be?

He ran out into the corridor, which was still empty. It seemed Henry wasn't having much luck getting people out of bed and up onto the deck.

George ran a little ways down the hall.

There!

He hurried down a bit farther.

Yes! Another lemon drop!

Phoebe! His smart sister!

Aunt Daisy came up behind him.

"She's left a trail of lemon drops," George said.

Aunt Daisy looked confused.

"Like Hansel and Gretel," George explained. "She left a trail so she could find her way back."

CHAPTER 10

George and Aunt Daisy scrambled to get dressed and put on their life jackets. Aunt Daisy brought Phoebe's warmest coat, and George carried the extra life jacket. They'd quickly find Phoebe and head up to the boat deck. And tomorrow morning this would be a big joke to laugh at over breakfast.

George thought that Phoebe had gone to the promenade deck—that she'd been woken up by the commotion with the ice and figured that George had gone out to see what was happening.

But when they got to the main staircase, he saw that the yellow glints were headed downstairs, not up to the deck.

His heart sank.

Phoebe had headed down to the first class baggage hold. Because she knew that George would want to see that mummy.

Of course she'd known.

Phoebe could read his mind.

A chill went through George's bones.

What if the scar-faced man was lurking in the baggage hold when Phoebe got there?

He ran faster down the stairs now. Aunt Daisy called after him, but he didn't slow down.

But when he got down to G deck, there was a gate stretched across the doorway.

"This wasn't here when I came down," he said to Aunt Daisy. He tried to pull it open, but it was locked. And just on the other side there was

a mob of people standing restlessly, third class passengers from the looks of their worn clothing.

"Look," Aunt Daisy said, pointing at one of Phoebe's candies glinting on the floor on the other side of the gate, pushed next to the wall. "She's down here. Pardon me!" she called to the steward standing in front of the crowd.

"You've gone the wrong way, madam," he said, staring at Aunt Daisy's huge diamond ring. "The captain wants first class passengers up on the boat deck now."

"My niece is down here somewhere," Aunt Daisy said. "You need to let us through."

"I'm sure she wouldn't have wandered down this far," the steward said.

"We're quite sure she's down here," Aunt Daisy said. "So if you'll please open the gate."

"I'm sorry, madam," he said. "Regulations . . ."

"Open this gate at once!" Aunt Daisy shouted in a tone George had never heard her use before.

The man took a key from his pocket and opened the gate. He stepped aside to let them pass. The crowd surged forward.

"Get back!" the steward shouted. "We'll tell you when it's time for you to go up!"

A few of the men lunged toward him.

Aunt Daisy grabbed George's arm.

The steward took a pistol from his pocket. His

hand shook as he waved it toward the crowd. George and Aunt Daisy stepped through the gate. The steward slammed it behind them.

They were trapped down there, just like everyone else.

George and Aunt Daisy squeezed through the crowd, weaving around trunks and stepping over sleeping children. There were so many people. If Phoebe's candies were down here, they couldn't see them anymore.

Suddenly something crashed into George from behind. A pair of arms wrapped around his waist so tightly he couldn't breathe.

George's heart stopped — the scar-faced man?

"GIORGIO!" Enzo screamed up at him.

George's eardrums nearly split in two.

Enzo's father hurried over to them. He tried to gently peel Enzo away from George.

But the little boy wouldn't let go.

"NO!" he howled. "NO!"

"Very sorry," Marco said, smiling apologetically

at Aunt Daisy, who looked more confused than ever. "We are old friends of Giorgio."

George started to introduce Aunt Daisy, but before he could get three words out, Enzo was dragging him down the hall, elbowing his way through the crowd like a pint-sized bull.

"See! See!" Enzo said.

"What?" George said. "No . . ."

"See! See!"

What was this kid doing? What did he want George to see?

The answer was just a few steps away, through an open doorway.

It was the mail sorting room.

Except now all George could see was water, green water swirling halfway up the stairs, foaming and churning like a stormy river. Sacks of mail bobbed up and down. Hundreds of letters floated on the surface.

And now George understood what Enzo was saying.

Sea.

The sea.

The *Titanic* was filling with water from the sea.

CHAPTER 11

Unsinkable.

Unsinkable.

George whispered those words like a prayer, over and over in his mind. He thought of Mr. Andrews, of how sure he was of this ship.

But the longer he stared at that water, that foaming green water, rising higher every second, the more certain he became: The *Titanic* was in trouble.

"We must go up," Marco said to Aunt Daisy. "We find a way."

But she shook her head, holding up Phoebe's bright blue coat and her life jacket.

"My niece, Phoebe," Aunt Daisy said. "She's down here. . . ."

George could see she was fighting back tears. George had never seen her look so sad and helpless, not even when Uncle Cliff died.

"She came down here looking for me," George said. "We can't find her."

Marco's amber eyes became very intent.

"An idea," he said. He knelt down and spoke to Enzo in Italian.

The boy smiled and nodded.

Then Marco hoisted the little boy up onto his shoulders.

Enzo took a huge breath and screamed,

"Phoebe!

"PHOEBE!"

People stopped talking and stared up at the boy with the foghorn voice.

"*Phoebe!*

"*PHOEBE!*"

As a hush fell over the crowd, George heard a faint voice.

"I'm here! I'm here!"

The crowd parted, and Phoebe appeared, her spectacles crooked, her face pale.

She staggered forward and threw her arms around George, burying her face in his chest.

"I found you," she whispered.

George didn't bother arguing over who did the finding. And anyway, his words were stuck in his throat. So he just held her tight.

It took some time for Phoebe to calm down enough to tell her story: that yes, she had been looking for George and heading for the baggage hold, that she got caught in the crowd of people rushing toward the back of the ship.

"It was like a stampede," she said.

As Phoebe talked, Aunt Daisy helped her into her coat and life jacket. Enzo held Phoebe's hand, like they were old friends. And the strange thing was that it felt that way, like they'd known Marco and Enzo forever. Maybe that's what happened when you got trapped in a flooding ship together.

George started to feel calmer with Phoebe close to him.

But then came a deep booming sound, a kind of groaning that echoed up all around them. At first George thought maybe the engines had started up again. But no, this wasn't the sound of the *Titanic*'s mighty engines.

The entire ship catapulted forward. People fell, toppling like dominoes. George was thrown into the wall. Screams and shouts echoed through the hallway. He managed to grab Enzo by the life jacket as he went sailing by him. Enzo just giggled as he fell into George's lap. To him this was a fun game. George hoped he never figured out that it wasn't.

"What was that?" Phoebe gasped, digging her fingers into George's arms.

Nobody answered.

But they all knew.

The *Titanic* was sinking.

"We will go up," Marco said.

"How?" Aunt Daisy said.

Phoebe grabbed George's hand.

"You, Georgie," she said.

"What?" George said.

"Phoebe's right," Aunt Daisy said. "You know the ship better than anyone." She turned to Marco. "He's explored every inch."

George couldn't believe it. They were counting on him?

But what if he made a mistake?

What if they all got lost?

"You can do it," Phoebe whispered.

And so George closed his eyes, picturing Mr. Andrews's blueprints in his mind.

And he remembered: the escape ladders.

He remembered what Mr. Andrews had told him: *The ladders are in the stokers' quarters, and they run up three decks.*

He pointed toward the front of the ship.

"This way," he said.

CHAPTER 12

There was no crowd here. Just abandoned trunks and suitcases.

And water. It was seeping into the hallway from under the doors of some of the cabins. No wonder those people were trying to push their way upstairs. They'd probably known right away that the ship was in trouble and the bottom decks were flooding.

The door to the stokers' quarters was locked.

Marco handed Enzo over to George and rammed the door with his shoulder, breaking the lock.

George rushed inside and went to the back wall.

And there it was, a ladder bolted to the wall. Just like Mr. Andrews said it would be. It came through the floor and shot straight up through an opening in the ceiling. George almost laughed with relief.

"Bravo, George!" Marco said.

"Bravo, Giorgio!" Enzo said, clapping.

George hopped up onto the ladder, with Phoebe and Aunt Daisy at his heels.

George was worried about Enzo, but the little guy scrambled like a monkey right ahead of Marco. They came up in a small dining room meant for crew members, and then George led everyone down a long second class corridor, up the grand staircase, and finally out onto the crowded boat deck.

They'd made it!

An officer came hurrying over to Aunt Daisy.

"Madam, there is a lifeboat about to leave. You and the children must come at once."

The man looked at Marco.

"Women and children only, sir," he said somberly. "I'm afraid you will have to stay with the other gentlemen."

Marco nodded. "Yes," he said. "I know."

Phoebe had been right. There weren't enough lifeboats. Not nearly enough.

What would happen to all of these men on deck? There were hundreds of them! And what about the crew? And those people down on G deck?

George's heart was pounding so hard he thought it would break through his chest.

He felt dizzy and sick.

Marco got down on his knees and spoke very quietly to Enzo.

Enzo nodded. Marco kissed him on the forehead, and then Enzo ran over to Aunt Daisy. She picked him up.

"I say he will go on a special boat ride," Marco said. "I say you will not leave him."

Aunt Daisy nodded, her eyes welling with tears.

"I promise you that."

Marco and Aunt Daisy looked at each other. Neither of them said a word, but a whole conversation seemed to happen with their eyes.

Phoebe was really crying now, looking away so Enzo wouldn't see. George felt like someone was choking him.

"Come on now!" the officer screamed.

And so they left Marco, and when George turned around just a few seconds later, he was gone.

The officer led them through a crowd of men to the side of the ship, where a lifeboat hung just over the side. It was packed with people, all women and children except for two sailors who stood at either end.

An officer helped Phoebe over the rail, and then one of the sailors reached over and pulled her into the boat. George helped Enzo, who tumbled in next to Phoebe. Aunt Daisy had a hard time climbing over in her skirts, but George held her hand, and she finally made it.

Now it was George's turn. As he took a step over the railing, someone pulled him back roughly.

"No more room," the officer said. "Women and children only. Lower away!" he called.

"No!" called Aunt Daisy, standing up in the boat. "He's only ten years old! Wait!"

The lifeboat rocked and almost tipped over. Ladies shrieked.

"You will drown us all!" a woman shouted.

"Sit down or I'll throw you over!" the sailor said.

And now Phoebe was screaming too.

Enzo howled.

George was too shocked to move.

Phoebe leaped up and grabbed hold of one of the ropes. She was trying to climb out of the lifeboat, back to George. He gasped as her hand slipped and she dangled over the sea. A sailor grabbed her around the waist and threw her into the boat.

And then the boat slid down on its ropes and splashed into the water.

Aunt Daisy and Phoebe were shouting up at him as the sailors rowed the boat away. George stood there at the rail, watching, his entire body shaking.

He stood there for what felt like a long time after their boat disappeared into the darkness.

He couldn't look down at the water, so he stared up at the sky, at all of those stars.

He closed his eyes and told himself it was a nightmare. He was really asleep in his suite. Or no, he was home on the farm, in his bed, with

Phoebe sleeping across the room and Papa sitting by the fire downstairs.

He closed his eyes tighter.

He tried to block out the terrible noises around him. He felt himself tipping to the side and he held tighter to the rail. And then he couldn't hold on anymore. His hand slipped.

And George fell, smashing his head on the deck.

And then there was silence.

CHAPTER 13

Strong arms lifted George up. He felt himself being carried.

"Papa?" he said. "Papa?"

Why did his head hurt so much? Had the panther knocked him out of the tree? Was he sick with a fever like Mama? And whose voice was whispering in his ear?

"Giorgio. Giorgio. Wake up."

George opened his eyes. Marco's amber eyes shone down on him.

This was no dream. He was not sick.

The *Titanic* was sinking.

The bow was completely underwater now, and waves swept over the deck. Lounge chairs sailed past them and crashed over the side. People clung to the rails. A few slipped and were swept overboard.

Marco had wrapped one arm around the railing and the other around George.

"It's time to go," Marco said.

"Go where?" George said, even though he knew.

They were going into the water. There was nowhere else for them to go.

Marco held George's arm as they climbed over the railing.

"When we jump, jump as far out as you can," Marco said. "Away from the ship."

George filled his lungs with the icy air.

"Jump!" Marco cried.

George pushed with his feet and leaped off the

boat. He closed his eyes, imagining that he had enormous wings that would take him soaring into the sky.

But then he hit the water, and down he went.

And just when he was sure his lungs would pop, the ocean seemed to spit him back up. George sputtered. The water was so cold it felt like millions of needles were stabbing him. It hurt so much he couldn't move.

Someone grabbed him by the life jacket and started dragging him away from the ship. It took George a few seconds to realize that it was Marco. He stopped to grab a door that was floating by. After helping George climb up on top, Marco found a crate for himself. It wasn't big enough to keep his feet out of the water. But it was better than nothing. The crate had a rope attached to it. Marco tied it around his arm and handed the end to George.

"Hold tight," he said.

They turned and stared at the ship.

The entire front was underwater, and the back had risen toward the sky. It groaned and squeaked and sparked. Black smoke poured from its funnels, and the lights flickered. It was like watching a fairy-tale dragon, stabbed and bleeding, fighting for its life.

And finally it seemed to give up.

The groaning stopped. The lights went dark. And the *Titanic* sank into the bubbling black water, down, down, down, down, until George closed his eyes.

He couldn't make himself watch Mr. Andrews's beautiful ship disappear.

A sound rose up around him, people calling for help. More and more people, screaming and yelling, hundreds of voices swirling together like a howling wind.

Marco pulled George away from the people and the wreckage. George couldn't believe how

strong he was, how hard he kicked, how his arms sliced through the water.

When he finally stopped, Marco was gasping for breath, exhaling cold clouds of white mist. He tightened the rope around his arm and patted George on the shoulder.

"I rest now, Giorgio," he said breathlessly. He closed his eyes and put his head down on the crate. "Soon."

Soon what? George was afraid to ask. Soon it would be over? Soon they would be rescued? Or soon they would be swallowed up by the darkness?

George heard men talking somewhere close by.

He looked around, relieved that he wasn't all by himself, and to his shock, just ahead, he saw a lifeboat.

"Marco!" he said. "Wake up!"

But Marco didn't move. His arms hung off the side of the crate. His feet dangled in the icy water.

"Marco! We need to get to that boat!"

But Marco was still. And George realized that his friend had used every last ounce of strength. He'd gotten George off the sinking ship, and across the icy waters.

It was up to George now.

He tucked the rope under his body and started paddling. The water seared his hands and arms. It was so cold it felt boiling hot, like lava.

But he didn't stop until he reached the boat.

It wasn't a regular wooden lifeboat. It was much smaller, and made of canvas cloth. There were about ten people crowded inside, mostly men. They all seemed dazed and frozen. Nobody spoke as George paddled up and grabbed hold of the side.

But somebody pushed his hand off.

"Get back," a voice said weakly. "You'll put us all in the water."

"Please," George said. "We need help."

George put his hand up again, but again someone pushed it off.

And so George pulled Marco to the other side of the boat. He tried again.

Nobody helped him. But this time nobody stopped him.

It took him three tries, but he managed to hoist himself over the side and tumble into the boat.

And now for Marco.

He got up on his knees and leaned over, bracing his legs against the side of the boat as he grabbed Marco under the arms. He pulled, but Marco was attached to the crate by the rope. He tried again, yanking the rope, digging at the knot with his frozen fingers. But the knot was like rusted metal. George struggled, and water sloshed over the side of the boat.

"Just let him go," one of the men said weakly. "It's hopeless."

But George kept working on the rope, trying now to break it away from the crate. He was pulling so hard that at first he didn't notice that Marco was slipping into the sea.

"Please! Somebody!" George screamed. "Can't you help us?"

A woman from the front of the boat climbed back to George.

She wore a black coat, her head and face hidden by a flowered shawl. As she pushed George aside she pulled something out of her coat.

A knife!

With a clean cut, she sliced the rope and helped George pull Marco into the boat.

Her hands looked surprisingly strong.

George fell back, exhausted.

"Thank you," George said to the woman through his chattering teeth.

The woman didn't say anything, and suddenly George noticed the knife. A bowie knife with an elk-horn handle.

George looked up, under the shawl. Two glittering blue eyes looked back at him.

The scar-faced man.

He had saved Marco's life.

Without a word, he handed George his knife.

Then he looked away.

CHAPTER 14

The cold pressed down on George until it seemed to crush his bones. He huddled close to Marco, trying to keep them both warm. Marco barely moved.

Some of the men sang softly.

Others prayed.

Some made no sounds at all.

Hours went by.

The sea became rougher, and every few minutes a wave splashed into the boat.

George was drifting off to sleep when one of the men shouted.

"It's a ship!"

And sure enough, a bright light was heading toward them.

"No," another man said. "It's just lightning."

But the light was getting bigger. And brighter.

George stared at that light, afraid that if he even blinked it would disappear, but soon he could see the outline of a gigantic ship steaming toward them.

He whispered to Marco, who barely fluttered his eyes. He pulled his friend closer, rubbing his arms.

"It won't be long," he whispered. "Hang on."

As the sky brightened, George gaped at the scene around him. It was as if they'd fallen through a hole in the ocean and come out on the other side of the earth.

There were icebergs all around them—hundreds of them, as far as George could see.

They sparkled in the golden pink light. They were so beautiful, but looking at them sent a chill up George's spine.

As the ship got closer, George could see that it was a passenger steamer, like the *Titanic*. Closer and closer it came, until George could read its name: *Carpathia*.

There were people crowded on the deck, looking over the rail. They were yelling and shouting and waving. But one voice rose above all the others, like a siren:

"PAPA! PAPA! GIORGIO!"

Marco's eyes fluttered, and he smiled a little.

"Enzo," he whispered.

George could see the little boy, waving frantically from Aunt Daisy's arms. Phoebe stood next to them, waving, with the sunlight glinting off her spectacles.

"They're safe, Marco!" George said. "They made it!"

George grabbed Marco's hand.

"And so did we."

CHAPTER 15

Those first two days on the *Carpathia* were a blur.

George mostly slept, on a bed of blankets and pillows on the floor of the first class lounge. But he sensed that Phoebe and Aunt Daisy never left his side. He sometimes heard Enzo singing softly to him in Italian, his breath hot on George's cheek. He heard Aunt Daisy and Phoebe talking—about Marco, whose feet were badly frozen, about the *Carpathia*'s passengers, who couldn't do enough for them all. About the hundreds and hundreds of people who didn't make it out of the water.

Slowly George felt stronger, and on their last night at sea, he was able to go out onto the deck with Phoebe.

They sat on a bench, wrapped in a blanket. A stewardess came over and gave them each a mug of warm milk.

Phoebe looked up at the sky as she warmed her hands on her mug.

"I finally saw a shooting star, when I was on the lifeboat," she said. "You can guess what I wished for."

George reached for her hand.

Yes, of course he knew.

On the bench next to them sat two women. Both were crying. Probably they'd lost their husbands. Or brothers. Or fathers.

There hadn't been enough wishing stars for everyone that night.

Phoebe said that only about 700 of them made it out of the water.

Phoebe leaned in close to George. Her coat smelled like rose water. A lady from the *Carpathia* had given it to her.

"Have you wondered?" she asked quietly, "if maybe there really was a curse?"

At first George didn't understand that Phoebe was talking about the mummy.

With all that had happened, George hadn't thought about it.

But now it hit him: how strange it was that the ship had collided with the iceberg at the exact moment the scar-faced man had opened the lid of Mr. Burrows's crate.

"I guess we'll never know," George said.

But the next evening, as the *Carpathia* was closing in on New York Harbor, George and Phoebe overheard a skinny man with a beard speaking to an officer.

"Before the *Titanic*, I was traveling in Egypt, a

place called Thebes," the man said. "I explored a magnificent tomb of a royal family."

Phoebe's eyes bugged out.

And before George could stop her, she had marched over to the man.

"Excuse me," she said. "Are you Mr. Burrows?"

"Yes, I am," the man replied.

Phoebe took a big breath.

"Mr. Burrows," she said. "This might sound like a very strange question. But did you bring a mummy on board the *Titanic*?"

The man looked at Phoebe.

"A mummy?" he said.

"Yes," she said. "We heard it was a princess."

Mr. Burrows's eyes were tired and sad.

But he smiled a little.

"My princess," he said. "Yes."

"So there *was* a mummy?" Phoebe exclaimed.

"No, child," he said. "One should never take a mummy from a tomb. That is very bad luck.

Princess was my cat. She passed away on my trip to Egypt. And so I had her . . . wrapped, so I could bring her back with me."

"So the princess was a cat?"

"Yes," he said sadly. "The most beautiful cat that ever lived."

Three hours later, just after nine o'clock, the *Carpathia* docked in New York City in a thunderstorm.

There were thousands of people waiting on the pier.

But the first person George saw as they walked down the gangplank was Papa. He rushed up to George and Phoebe, grabbing them both and pulling them to him. All around them, people cried with happiness. Others just cried, their tears mixing with the pouring rain.

They introduced Papa to Marco and Enzo, but there wasn't much time to talk. Their train to

Millerstown was leaving soon, and an ambulance was waiting to take Marco to the hospital.

Luckily, George didn't have to say a real goodbye to Marco and Enzo.

Aunt Daisy was staying in New York City to take care of Enzo until Marco's feet were healed. And then they would come with her for a visit to Millerstown. Seeing the way Marco and Aunt Daisy were looking at each other, George wondered if maybe Marco and Enzo would stay forever. George sure hoped so.

As they rode to the train station, newsboys screamed from every street corner.

"Read all about it! Titanic survivors in New York! More than fifteen hundred people dead! Read all about it!"

George covered his ears.

He wanted to forget everything about the *Titanic*.

He wanted to put it out of his mind forever.

CHAPTER 16

But he couldn't forget.

Even back on the farm, surrounded by friends from school and neighbors from town, he felt like he was still drifting on the dark ocean. And each day that went by, he felt himself drifting farther away. At night, when he got into bed, he'd see the faces of all those scared people on G deck. He'd see the ship disappearing into the sea. He'd remember the stabbing cold, and the screams of hundreds of people crying for help.

He didn't bother trying to fall asleep. Each night, after Phoebe and Papa were in bed, he went out into the woods.

He was heading back to the house one night when he heard a noise through the bushes.

Something was there. He could sense it.

The panther?

He took out his knife, fighting the urge to run away, and peered through the branches.

George stared in shock.

It was Papa.

He was sitting on a large rock, looking up at the sky, smoking his pipe. He looked like he'd been there for some time.

Papa turned. He didn't look especially surprised to see George.

"Sorry to give you a scare," he said.

"What are you doing here?" George asked.

"Don't know," Papa said. "Sometimes I just come here, when I can't sleep."

George couldn't believe it. How many nights

had they both been out in the woods at the same time?

Papa eased himself off the rock and began walking back toward the house. "I'll take you up to your bed."

"No, Papa," George said. "I come to the woods too."

Papa looked at him with a very slight smile.

"I know that," he said.

Papa knew? What else did Papa know about George?

What else *didn't* George know about Papa?

He and his father looked at each other. Really looked, for the first time in a long while, maybe since Mama died.

Suddenly George started to cry. They took him by surprise, his tears, and he couldn't stop. He cried for all those people who didn't make it out of the water. He cried because somehow he did. He cried because he knew that no matter how much time went by, a part of him would still be out in that ocean. He would never forget.

Papa held George's hand and didn't say a word. And then he led George over to the boulder, where they sat together under the stars.

George stared up at the sky. Were those really the same stars that had burned so brightly above the black ocean that night?

Was he really still the same boy?

George, who couldn't stay out of trouble. George, who didn't try hard at school.

George, who found the escape ladders. George, who pulled Marco to that lifeboat.

Who didn't give up.

They sat on the boulder for a long while, and as the sun started to peep over the trees, George told Papa about Mr. Andrews.

"He said he thought one day I'd build a ship."

Papa didn't laugh. He puffed on his pipe, looking thoughtful.

"How about we build one together?" Papa said. "A nice little boat. For the pond. I've always wanted to do that."

"That's a good idea," George said.

A great idea.

"We could start today," Papa said, standing up and holding out his hand.

They walked back to the house together. The birds were singing softly. The chickens were squawking for breakfast. A breeze was whispering through the trees. And a voice seemed to sing to George, very softly:

"Awake, awake.
It's now daybreak!
But don't forget your dreams. . . ."

Papa looked out into the woods, like he could hear it too.

MY *TITANIC* STORY

This book is a work of historical fiction. That means that all of the facts about the *Titanic* are true, but the main characters came from my imagination. George, Phoebe, Aunt Daisy, Marco, and Enzo are based on people I learned about while researching the *Titanic*. By the time I finished writing this book, they sure felt real to me.

I can see George now, relaxing in the little boat he and Papa built, rowing around their pond while Phoebe watches from the shore, reading a book about dinosaur fossils. I can picture Aunt Daisy and Marco's wedding, how Enzo would run down the aisle with a huge grin on his face. That's my favorite part of being a writer, giving my characters happiness in the end. If only I could do the same for the 1,517 people who didn't survive the sinking of the *Titanic*.

What a sad and terrible story!

One day as I was trying to finish the book, I needed a break, so I went to New York City with my eleven-year-old son, Dylan. We stopped to rest in one of my favorite neighborhoods, in a tiny park on West 106th Street and Broadway with trees and a bronze statue of a woman lying on her side. I read the gold writing engraved in a marble bench, and to my surprise I saw that the entire park was a memorial to two famous New Yorkers who died on the *Titanic*, Isidor and Ida Straus.

I couldn't forget the *Titanic*, it seemed, not even for an afternoon.

And nearly one hundred years later, the world hasn't forgotten either.

FACTS ABOUT THE *TITANIC*

More has been written about the *Titanic* than any other disaster in modern history. I tried to include as much information as I could in the book. But here are some more amazing facts that I wanted to share with you.

- The *Titanic* was the largest ship—the largest moving object—ever built. It weighed close to 50,000 tons, and was eleven stories tall and four city blocks long.

- There were 2,229 people on board—1,316 passengers and 913 crew. Survivors included 498 passengers and 215 members of the crew.

- The passengers came from 28 different countries, including many from America, England, Ireland, and

Finland. There were a few passengers
from China, Japan, Mexico, and South
Africa. Most of the crew members were
from England and Ireland.

- There were nine dogs on the *Titanic*.
  They stayed in kennels, but their
  owners could take them out onto the
  decks for walks. Two Pomeranians and
  one Pekingese survived with their
  masters.

- After the sinking of the *Titanic*, laws
  were changed to require all ships
  to carry enough lifeboats for every
  passenger and crew member.

- For decades, divers, scientists, and
  treasure hunters searched for the
  wreck of the *Titanic*. It was finally
  located in 1985 by a team led by U.S.
  scientist Robert Ballard, 2 1/2 miles
  below the surface of the sea.

- Ballard and his team did not take anything from the wreck. Dr. Ballard believes the *Titanic* should rest in peace as a memorial to those who died. But he couldn't stop treasure hunters from diving to the wreck and removing thousands of artifacts: jewelry, dishes, clothes, even the ship's hull.

What do you think about this? Do you think the *Titanic* should be brought to the surface or left in peace?

Lauren Tarshis at the Isidor and Ida Straus Titanic *memorial in New York City.*   PHOTO BY DAVID DREYFUSS

Lauren Tarshis's *New York Times* bestselling I Survived series tells stories of young people and their resilience and strength in the midst of unimaginable disasters and times of turmoil. Lauren has brought her signature warmth, integrity, and exhaustive research to topics such as the September 11 attacks, the American Revolution, Hurricane Katrina, the bombing of Pearl Harbor, and other world events. Lauren lives in Connecticut with her family, and can be found online at laurentarshis.com.

THE ASSEMBLY LINE

by

Robert Linhart

translated by Margaret Crosland

The University of Massachusetts Press
AMHERST, 1981

First published in the USA 1981 by
The University of Massachusetts Press
PO Box 429, Amherst, Massachusetts 01004

This translation copyright © 1981 John Calder (Publishers) Ltd

Published in Great Britain 1981 by
John Calder (Publishers) Ltd
Originally published in France 1978 as
L'établi, by Les Editions de Minuit

Copyright © 1978 by Editions de Minuit

Library of Congress Cataloging in Publication Data

Linhart, Robert.
  The assembly line.
  Translation of: L'établi.
  1. Automobile industry workers — France — Case studies.
  2. Industrial relations — France — Case studies.
  3. Assembly-line methods—Case studies. I. Title.

HD8039.A82F7313   331.7'629222'0944   81-1703
ISBN 0-87023-322-X (pbk.)   AACR2

Photoset in 11/12pt Baskerville in Great Britain
Printed and Bound in the United Kingdom.

CONTENTS

Introduction

In the spring of 1968 the Left Bank of Paris, site of most university activity and the center of French intellectual life, exploded into revolution. De Gaulle had been in power for ten years, brought out of retirement to spearhead the determination of the Algerian white settlers to keep their colony French in spite of the increasing sympathy of the French public for the sufferings of the Algerians during the long war of attrition against the FLN, the liberation army. The Algerian war strengthened both the extreme Left and the extreme Right in France, and most leaders of opinion, popular writers, actors, and journalists, alarmed by the increasing stories of torture and atrocity coming from Algiers, sided with the Left and the FLN. But de Gaulle, brought suddenly to power by the Right and nervously accepted by the Right-Center parties fearful of civil war, surprised everyone by turning against the very people who had acclaimed him as their savior in Algiers. His famous remark, "Je vous ai compris," taken to mean that he was solidly with the white colonists, meant in fact that he had understood that no peace was possible in Algeria except by French withdrawal, and he rapidly brought the war to an end, subverted a military *coup d'état* against him, and imposed a strong personal presidential rule on the country.

By so doing he incurred the emnity of Left and Right, although supported by the great bulk of the French bourgeoisie and peasantry. The Right hated him because he had betrayed them in Algeria and the Left because they saw in his authoritarianism their permanent exclusion from power, except by revolution. The students were solidly anti-Gaullist and accustomed to frequent clashes with the police, who, after many years of dealing with Algerian dissidents and communist demonstrations, were savage when in action. It was the students who created the revolution of 1968: coming initially from the faculties of arts and humanities in the main, inspired by the heady glamor of French history—1789, 1848, 1871: dates commemorated not just by the history books, but by the mainstream of French artistic creation in painting, literature, and music—students found themselves with a heaven-sent opportunity to relive their glorious past, and the paving stones of Paris were torn up to build barricades. The area around the Sorbonne became a heavily defended citadel in which the students were soon joined by armies of political sympathizers and large numbers of poets, painters, and intellectuals, who together successfully repulsed police attempts to break through. Much of the publicity went to flamboyant personalities like Jean-Jacques Lebel, who occupied the Odéon, one of France's most famous national theaters, then under the direction of Jean-Louis Barrault, where daily debates and forums were held. But there was a hard core of militant leftist intellectuals interested not in the excitement, but in creating a real revolution to totally change French society, of whom the best-known was Danny Cohn-Bendit ("Danny le rouge"). This core included the group who called themselves "the establishment". When the student rising was finally put down by the army under General Massu, who ten years earlier had been one of the leaders of the *coup* against de Gaulle, it was this group that, analyzing their failure, decided that it was the indifference and nonparticipation of the workers which had prevented the revolution from spreading and succeeding. Robert Linhart, the author of this book, was one of the establishment group.

He decided to go to work at the Citroën factory at Choisy, enrolling as a worker and hiding the fact that he was university educated and qualified to teach. He was taken on as an ordinary unqualified worker and, because he was white and French, was immediately graded above the Blacks, Arabs, and East Europeans who made up the bulk of the work force. He learned the reality of working on the assembly line and what it involves in terms of relentless and dangerous hard labor, loss of dignity and individuality, victimization and exploitation. Although the author went into the factory in order to learn about working conditions and to politicize the workers, he had no idea what working conditions were really like and his horror at the discovery is documented in this book objectively and with an economic style that graphically conveys the realities of a mass production factory.

The French title, *L'Etabli*, has a double meaning: it refers to the "establishment" to which the author belonged and also to a place of work in a factory, because *L'Etabli* is also the work bench where an old worker repairs damaged car doors, taken off the assembly line before they are returned to production. The enormous success of the original French edition of *The Assembly Line*, which has been a subject of conversation in France since its publication in 1978, proves what little knowledge and understanding most concerned middle-class people have of routine factory labor and its effect on the human personality. Never before has factory work been so minutely and poignantly described, and the principal importance of this book lies in the lessons that can be learned from that description.

One of the major problems of Western capitalist society concerns work. Unemployment is endemic in third-world countries and forces the young generations of unindustrialized countries to travel abroad to find any work they can in factories or on the land. In times of recession even the industrial nations cannot employ their own people and competition for jobs breeds conflict, racism, and exploitation. It is the nature of mass production to overproduce, thereby deepening recession, and one of the great anomalies of capitalism is that it produces poverty in the midst of plenty every time the pendulum swings toward its nadir. In recent years an increasing number of thoughtful people have looked nostalgically at life before the industrial revolution, even though it was similar to existing conditions in third-world countries today. No politician or economist dares suggest a return to a nonindustrial society based on specialization and crafts-manship, where goods are made to last, but world shortages of raw materials will inevitably bring most mass production to a stop one day. But then there is the other great problem: population. Every responsible forecast predicts mass starvation in this century, with populations growing ever larger, which makes any return to the simple life impossible in civilized terms. There is an answer in decimation by war or plague, but it cannot be contemplated by any humane person. *The Assembly Line* does not go into these problems, but the implications are clear from the circumstances that drive so many desperate workers toward Citroën.

What is also clear is that assembly line work under conditions such as are described here should have no place in a civilized democracy. The nature of the work itself is destructive to health, reasonable existence, and human dignity. It can only breed conflict through strikes, sabotage, and ultimately violence. It is easier to understand why demands that often seem outrageous are made by factory workers, and why there is such deep distrust of management, after reading Robert Linhart's book. This is not to say that things are necessarily any better in the peoples' republics of Eastern Europe, where factory work can be little different and the "official" state-run unions are little different from the "yellow" union at Citroën.

I take the view that bad working conditions indicate bad and insensitive management, and that—although the kind of mass production described here, where the humiliation of the worker is a necessary part of the system to get ever more production at ever less cost, is always to be condemned—mass production will continue nevertheless, and that reforms can and must be introduced to bring a measure of conviviality, as well as interest and dignity, into such work. But this book, painfully convincing and moving in the directness of its narrative, is designed above all to start each of us thinking individually about the human cost of those things that we buy and enjoy ... and how to diminish that cost.

John Calder

1

The first day: Mouloud

"Show him, Mouloud."

The man in the white overalls (he's the foreman, called Gravier, as they'll tell me later) leaves me standing and goes off busily toward his glass-walled cage.

I look at the laborer who is working. I look at the shop floor. I look at the assembly line. No one speaks to me. Mouloud takes no notice of me. The foreman has gone. So I observe at random: Mouloud, the Citroën 2 CV car bodies passing in front of us, and the other laborers.

The assembly line isn't as I'd imagined it. I'd visualized a series of clear-cut stops and starts in front of each work position: with each car moving a few yards, stopping, the worker doing his job, the car starting again, another one stopping, the same operation being carried out again, etc. I saw the whole thing taking place rapidly—with those "diabolical rhythms" mentioned in the leaflets. *The assembly line*: the words themselves conjured up a jerky, rapid flow of movement.

The first impression, on the contrary, is one of a slow but continuous movement by all the cars. The operations themselves seem to be carried out with a kind of resigned monotony, but without the speed I expected. It's like a long, gray-green, gliding movement, and after a time it gives off a feeling of somnolence, interrupted by sounds, bumps, flashes of light, all repeated one after the other, but with regularity. The formless music of the line, the gliding movement of the unclad gray steel bodies, the routine movements: I can feel myself being gradually enveloped and anesthetized. Time stands still.

Three sensations form the boundaries of this new universe. The smell: an acrid odor of scorched metal and metallic dust. The sound: the drills, the roaring of the blow torches, the hammer strokes on metal. And the grayness: everything's gray, the walls of the shop, the metallic bodies of the 2 CVs, the overalls and work clothes that the men wear. Even their faces look gray, as though the pale, greenish light from the cars passing in front of them were imprinted on their features.

The soldering shop, where I've just been allocated ("Put him to watch number 86," the sector manager had said) is fairly small. Thirty positions or so, arranged around a semicircular line. The cars arrive as nailed-up sections of coachwork, just pieces of metal joined together: here the steel sections have to be soldered, the joints eliminated and covered up; the object which leaves the workshop is still a gray skeleton, a car body, but a skeleton looking from now on as if it's all in one piece. The body is now ready for the chemical coatings, painting, and the rest of the assembly.

I note each stage of the work.

The position at the entrance to the shop is manned by a worker with special lifting gear. We're on the first floor, or rather a kind of mezzanine floor with only one wall. Each car body is attached to a rope, and the man drops it—roughly—onto a platform at the start of the assembly line. He secures the platform to one of the big hooks you can see moving slowly at ground level, a yard or two apart. These hooks make up the visible part of the perpetual motion mechanism: "the assembly line". Beside this worker stands a man in blue overalls supervising the start of the line, and he intervenes from time to time to speed things up: "O.K., that's it, fix it on now!" Several times during the day I'll see him at this spot, urging the man with the lifting gear to get more cars into the circuit. They'll tell me later that he's Antoine, the charge hand. He's a Corsican, small and excitable. "He makes a lot of noise, but he's not bad. The thing is, he's afraid of Gravier, the foreman."

The crash of a new car body arriving every three or four minutes marks out the rhythm of the work.

As soon as the car has been fitted into the assembly line it begins its half-circle, passing each successive position for soldering or another complementary operation, such as filing, grinding, hammering. As I said, it's a continuous movement and it looks slow: when you first see the line it almost seems to be standing still, and you've got to concentrate on one actual car in order to realize that car is moving, gliding progressively from one position to the next. Since nothing stops, the workers also have to move in order to stay with the car for the time it takes to carry out the work. In this way each man has a well-defined area for the operations he has to make, although the boundaries are invisible: as soon as a car enters a man's territory, he takes down his blowtorch, grabs his soldering iron, takes his hammer or his file, and gets to work. A few knocks, a few sparks, then the soldering's done and the car's already on its way out of the three or four yards of this position. And the next car's already coming into the work area. And the worker starts again. Sometimes, if he's been working fast, he has a few seconds' respite before a new car arrives: either he takes advantage of it to breathe for a moment, or else he intensifies his effort and "goes up the line" so that he can gain a little time, in other words, he works further ahead, outside his normal area, together with the worker at the preceding position. And after an hour or two he's amassed the incredible capital of two or three minutes in hand, that he'll use up smoking a cigarette, looking on like some comfortable man of means as his car moves past already soldered, keeping his hands in his pockets while the others are working. Short-lived happiness: the next car's already there: he'll have to work on it at his usual position this time, and the race begins again, in the hope of gaining one or two yards, "moving up" in the hope of another peaceful cigarette. If, on the other hand, the worker's too slow, he "slips back", that is, he finds himself carried progressively beyond his position, going on with his work when the next laborer has already begun his. Then he has to push on fast, trying to catch up. And the slow gliding of the cars, which seems to me so near to not moving at all, looks as relentless as a rushing torrent which you can't manage to dam up: eighteen inches, three feet, thirty seconds certainly behind time, this awkward join, the car followed too far, and the next one already appearing at the usual starting point of the station, coming forward with its mindless regularity and its inert mass. It's already halfway along before you're able to touch it, you're going to start on it when it's nearly passed through and reached the next station: all this loss of time mounts up. It's what they call "slipping" and sometimes it's as ghastly as drowning.

I'll learn this assembly line existence later, as the weeks go by. On the first day I must get the hang of it: through the tension on a face, some irritable gesture, the anxiety in a man's glance toward a car body that's appearing when the one before is not yet finished. As I look at the laborers one after another I'm beginning to see differences in what seemed at first glance to be a homogeneous human mechanism: one man is calm and precise, another sweats from overwork; I notice that some are ahead, some are behind; I see the minute, tactical details at each station, the men who put their tools down between cars and those who hold onto them, those who get out of step ... And the perpetual, slow, implacable gliding of the 2 CVs under construction, minute by minute, movement by movement, operation by operation. The punch. The sparks. The drills. Scorched metal.

Once the car body has finished its circuit at the end of the curving line it's taken off its platform and pushed into a moving tunnel which takes it off to the paint shop. And there's the crash of a new car coming on the line to replace it.

Through the gaps in this gray, gliding line I can glimpse a war of attrition, death versus life and life versus death. Death: being caught up in the line, the imperturbable gliding of the cars, the repetition of identical gestures, the work that's never finished. If one car's done, the next one isn't, and it's already there, unsoldered at the precise spot that's just been done, rough at the precise spot that's just been polished. Has the soldering been done? No, it's waiting. Has it been done once and for all this time? No, it's got to be done again, it's always waiting to be done, it's never done—as though there were no more movement, no result from the movements, no change, only a ridiculous illusion of work which would be undone as soon as it's finished under the influence of some curse. And suppose you said to yourself that nothing matters, that you need only get used to making the same movements in the same way in the same period of time, aspiring to no more than the placid perfection of a machine? A temptation to death. But life kicks against it and resists. The organism resists. The muscles resist. The nerves resist. Something, in the body and the head, braces itself against repetition and nothingness. Life shows itself in more rapid movement, an arm lowered at the wrong time, a slower step, a second's irregularity, an awkward gesture, getting ahead, slipping back, tactics at the station; everything, in the wretched square of resistance against the empty eternity of the work station, indicates that there are still human incidents, even if they're minute; there's still time, even if it's dragged out to abnormal lengths. This clumsiness, this unnecessary movement away from routine, this sudden acceleration, this soldering that's gone wrong, this hand that has to do it all over again, the man who makes a face, the man who's out of step, this shows that life is hanging on. It is seen in everything that yells silently within every man on the line, "I'm not a machine!"

In fact, two stations beyond Mouloud, a worker—another Algerian, but more obviously so, he looks almost Asiatic—is in the process of "slipping". He's been gradually moving down toward the next station. He's getting nervous about his four bits of soldering. I can see him becoming more agitated, I can see the rapid movement of the blowtorch. All of a sudden he's had enough. He calls out to the charge hand, "Hey, not so fast, stop them a minute, it's no good like this!" And he unhooks the platform from the car he's working on, keeping it still as far as the next hook which will carry it forward again a few seconds later. The men working at the preceding stations unhook in their turns, to avoid a pile-up of cars. Everyone breathes for a moment. It makes a gap of a few yards in the line—a space a little bigger than the others—but the Algerian has caught up. This time Antoine, the section manager, says nothing: he's been pushing hard for an hour, and he's three or four cars in advance. But on other occasions he intervenes, gets after the man who's slipping back, won't let him unhook the car, or, if he's already done so, he rushes up to get the platform back to its original place.

This incident had to happen before I realized how tight the time schedule is. Yet the movement of the cars seems slow, and as a rule there's no sign of haste in the movements made by the workers.

So here I am at the factory. "Settled in." Being taken on was easier than I imagined. I'd thought out my story carefully: worked as a clerk in a grocery store owned by an imaginary uncle in Orléans, then storekeeper for a year (work certificate by special dispensation), military service with the engineers at Avignon (I gave the service record of a worker friend of mine of my own age and pretended I'd lost my record book). No diplomas, no, not even the BEPC. I could pass for a Parisian of provincial origin at loose ends in the capital, reduced to working in a factory because the family had lost all its money. I answered the questions briefly; I was silent and anxious. My wretched expression should not look out of place among the general appearance of the new intake. I hadn't put on the expression: the troubles of May 1968 and after—a summer of upset and quarrels—still showed on my worn face, just as others among my companions showed visibly the harsh conditions in which they lived. You feel right down when you come to beg for a little manual job—just enough money for food, please—and you timidly reply "none" to the questions about diplomas and qualifications, about anything special you can do. All my comrades in the job line were immigrants and I could read in their eyes the humiliations of this "none". As for me, I looked sufficiently wretched to seem like a would-be worker who was beyond suspicion. The man in charge of the new intake must have thought, "Yes, here's a fellow from the country, he's a bit dazed, really, that's good, he won't make any trouble." And he gave me my pass for the medical examination. Next please. And in any case, why should there be any complication about taking on a worker for the assembly line? That notion's typical of an intellectual who's used to complex appointments, a list of degrees, and "job analyses". That's what it's like when you're somebody. But if you're nobody ... Everything moves very fast here: it's easy to assess two arms! A lightning medical inspection, with the little gang of immigrants. A few movements of the muscles. X-ray. You're weighed. The atmosphere's there already: "Stand there," "Strip to the waist!" "Hurry up over there!" A doctor makes a few marks on a form. That's all, O.K. to work for Citroën. Next please.

It's a good moment: just now, in early September 1968, Citroën's devouring workers. Production's high and they're filling the gaps left among the immigrants by the month of August: some have not returned from their remote holidays, others will come back late and will learn to their despair that they've been fired ("We don't believe a damn word of it, that story about your old mother being ill, rubbish!") and already replaced. They replace people at once. In any case Citroën works in a state of flux: quickly in, quickly out. Average employment period at Citroën: a year. "A high turnover," say the sociologists. In fact, it's quick march. And for me there's no problem: I'm caught up in the flood of new entrants.

I left the recruitment office at Javel on Friday with a document: allocated to the plant at the Porte de Choisy.

"Go to the section manager on Monday morning at seven o'clock." And now, this Monday morning, the Citroën 2 CVs moving past in the soldering shop.

Mouloud still doesn't say anything. I watch him work. It doesn't look too difficult. On each car shell arriving, the metal parts which form the curve over the windshield have been lined up and nailed into position but there's a gap between them. Mouloud's job is to get rid of this gap. In this left hand he takes the tin, which is shiny; in his right, a blow torch. A flame bursts for a moment. Part of the tin melts in a little heap of soft stuff on the joint between the sheets of metal: Mouloud carefully spreads this stuff out, using a little stick which he picks up as soon as he puts the torch down. The crack disappears: the metal section above the windshield now looks as if it's all one piece. Mouloud has been alongside the car for two yards; when the job's done he leaves it and returns to his station, to wait for the next one. Mouloud works fast enough to have a few seconds free between cars, but he doesn't use the time to "move up". He prefers to wait. Here's a new car now. Shiny tin, blow torch, little stick, a few strokes to the left, to the right, up and down ... Mouloud walks along as he works on the car. A final stroke with the stick and the soldering's smooth. Mouloud comes back toward me. A new car approaches. No, it doesn't look too difficult: why doesn't he let me have a go?

The line stops. The men take out their snacks. "Break," Mouloud tells me, "it's quarter past eight." Is that all? I felt that hours had gone by in this gray shop, divided between the monotonous gliding of the car bodies and the dim flares from the blow torches. This interminable flow of sheet iron and metal outside time: only an hour and a quarter?

Mouloud offers me a share of the bread that he's carefully unwrapped from a piece of newspaper. "No, thanks. I'm not hungry."

"Where are you from?"

"Paris."

"Is this your first job with Citroën?"

"Yes, and my first time in a factory."

"I see. I'm from Kabylia. I've got a wife and children out there."

He takes out his wallet and shows me a faded family photograph. I tell him that I know Algeria. We talk about the winding roads in Greater Kabylia and the sheer cliffs which drop down to the sea near Collo. The ten minutes are up. The line starts again. Mouloud takes his blowtorch and goes toward the first approaching car.

We go on talking, intermittently, between cars.

"For the time being you only have to watch," Mouloud tells me. "You see, the soldering's done with tin. The 'stick' is made of tin. You have to get into the way of using it: if you put too much tin, it makes a lump on the coachwork and that's no good. If you don't put enough tin it doesn't fill up the hole and that's no good either. Watch what I do; you can try it this afternoon." And, after a silence: "You'll start soon enough ..."

And we talk about Kabylia, Algeria, olive growing, the rich Mitidja plain, tractors and ploughing, variations in the harvest, and the little mountain village where Mouloud's family has remained. He sends three hundred francs a month, and he's careful not to spend too much on himself. This month it's difficult, an Algerian workmate has died, and the others have subscribed to pay for sending the body back home, and a little money for the family, too. It's made a hole in Mouloud's budget, but he's proud of the solidarity among the Algerians and especially among the Kabylians. "We support each other like brothers."

Mouloud must be about forty. A small moustache, hair graying at the temples, a slow, calm voice. He speaks as he works, with precision and regularity. No unnecessary gestures. No unnecessary words.

The car bodies go by, Mouloud does his soldering. Torch, tin, piece of wood. Torch, tin, piece of wood.

A quarter past twelve. The canteen. Three-quarters of an

hour to eat. When I come back to my place, just before one o'clock, Mouloud's already there. I'm glad to see his face again, already familiar in the midst of this dirty gray workshop, this colorless metal.

It isn't one o'clock yet: they're waiting for work to start again. A little farther on a crowd has formed around the Algerian worker with the Asiatic features whom I saw "slipping back" this morning. "Hey, Sadok, let's have a look! Where did you get it?" I go closer. Sadok is cheerfully showing everyone a pornographic magazine, from Denmark or somewhere like that. The cover shows a girl sucking an erect penis. It's a close-up, in aggressive, realistic colors. I find it very ugly but Sadok seems delighted. He bought it from one of the truckdrivers who work for Citroën, transporting sheets of metal, engines, spare parts, containers, and finished cars, and who at the same time bring into the factory small supplies of cigars, cigarettes, and various other things.

Mouloud, who has taken in the cause of all this excitement with one glance, doesn't move. Someone calls out to him: "Hey, Mouloud, come and see a bit of rump, it'll do you good." He doesn't move, replies: "I'm not interested." And when I come back to join him he tells me in a lower voice: "It's not good. I've got a wife and kids out there in Kabylia. It's different for Sadok. He's a bachelor, he can amuse himself."

The porn magazine among the metallic dust and the filthy gray overalls: a painful impression. Prisoners' fantasies. I'm glad Mouloud stays away.

A metallic noise, everyone goes back to his place, the line starts to move again.

"Now it's your turn," Mouloud tells me. "You've seen what you've got to do." And he hands me the blowtorch and the tin.

"No, no! Not like that! And put the gloves on, you'll burn yourself. Whoa! mind the torch! Give it to me! ..."

This is the tenth car I've fenced with in vain. Mouloud

warns me, guides my hand, passes me the tin, holds the torch for me, all in vain; I can't do it.

On one car I flood the metal with tin because I've held the torch too near the tin and for too long: all Mouloud can do is scrape it all off and re-do the operation rapidly while the car has already almost left our area. Then I don't put on enough tin and the first touch with the little piece of wood merely shows up the crack again that had to be covered. And when by some miracle I've put more-or-less the right amount of tin, I spread it so clumsily—damn that little piece of wood that my fingers obstinately refuse to control!—that the soldering's as bumpy as a fairground switchback and there's a horrible lump where Mouloud succeeded in producing a perfectly smooth curve.

I get mixed up about the order of operations: you have to put the gloves on to hold the torch, take them off to use the little piece of wood, not touch the burning tin with your bare hands, hold the "stick" with your left hand, the torch in your right hand, the little piece of wood in your right hand, the gloves you've just taken off in your left hand, with the tin. It looked obvious when Mouloud did it, with a succession of precise, coordinated movements. I can't manage it, I panic: I nearly burn myself ten times over and Mouloud moves rapidly to push the torch away.

Every one of my joints has to be redone. Mouloud takes the instruments from me and just manages to catch up, three yards farther on. I'm sweating and Mouloud's beginning to get tired: his rhythm has been interrupted. He shows no impatience and continues to do this double work—guiding mine, and then re-doing it—but we're slipping back. We're moving inexorably down toward the next position, we're starting the next car one yard too late, then two yards; we finish it, or rather Mouloud finishes it, rapidly, three or four yards farther on, with the torch cable stretched almost to the limit, in the middle of the instruments belonging to the next position. The faster I try to go, the more I panic: I let the molten tin drip all over, I drop the little piece of wood, as I turn round the flame from my torch nearly gets Mouloud, he just manages to avoid it.

"No, not like that, now look!" There's nothing to be done. My fingers are awkward, I'm incurably clumsy. I'm wearing myself out. My arms are trembling. I press too hard with the wood, I can't control my hands, drops of sweat are beginning to get in my eyes. The car bodies seem to move at a frantic speed, there's no hope of getting ahead, Mouloud's finding it harder and harder to catch up.

"Now listen, getting in a state doesn't help. Stop a minute and watch what I do."

Mouloud takes the instruments from me and picks up the regular rhythm of his work again, a bit faster than before, in order gradually to make good the time we've lost: a few inches on each car; after ten or so he's almost back in his normal place. As for me, I get my breath back as I watch him work. His movements look so natural! What have his hands got that mine haven't? A car comes: tin, torch, piece of wood, and at the spot where the curving metal was split there's now a perfectly smooth surface. Why can he do the work and I can't?

The 3:15 break. Mouloud sacrifices it to me. The others stretch their legs, form groups, chat, come and go, sit on barrels, or lean against the cars which are standing still. Mouloud begins to explain again. The car in front of our position isn't moving, it's easier. That's the distance at which you hold the torch. And this is how you place your fingers on the stick. There. Press with your thumb to grasp the round part of the metal. In the middle you must press very lightly in order to stop the tin from escaping and you must press more and more firmly as you move away: that's how you get the graded effect. Take the wood to the left first, then to the right. Then a short stroke upward, and another downward. Mouloud repeats the movement slowly: four times, five times. My turn now: he guides my hand, arranges my fingers against the wood. Like that. There. Good, perhaps that'll be all right ... My brain thinks it understands it all: will my hands obey?

End of the break, back to work. Din of the line. A new car

comes forward, slow and menacing: I've got to carry out those movements again with the real thing. Quick, the torch, oh no! I forgot, the gloves first, where's the tin? Good God, how quickly it's coming, it's in the middle of our station already, use the torch, blast! too much tin, get rid of it with the piece of wood, it's gone all over ... Mouloud removes it for me with his hands. One more try ... No, it's no good. I'm dismayed, I must have looked at Mouloud in despair, he tells me: "Don't worry now, it's always a bit hard at first, have a rest, let me do it." Once more I stand on the edge, watching helplessly: the line has rejected me. And yet it seems to move so slowly ...

Mouloud decides not to give me the tools again.

"It'll go better tomorrow, go on now, you mustn't worry about it." We talk about his own beginnings at this station, a long time ago: he got the hang of it fairly quickly, but at first it's not easy ... By now he's had long experience with soldering and he does it mechanically.

In fact I've heard that soldering is a craft. What qualifications has Mouloud got? I ask him how Citroën classifies him. "M2," he replies in laconic fashion. Laborer.

I'm astonished. He's only a laborer? Yet soldering's not as easy as all that. I can't do anything, but I've been taken on as a "semiskilled worker" (OS2, says the contract): in the hierarchy of the not-very-important, semiskilled is still above laborer ... Mouloud obviously doesn't want to go places. I don't say anything more. As soon as I can I'll find out on what principles Citroën makes their classifications. A few days later another worker told me. There are six categories of nonqualified workers. Starting at the bottom: three categories of laborers (M1, M2, M3); three categories of semiskilled workers (OS1, OS2, OS3). The distinction is made in a perfectly simple way: it's racist. The Blacks are M1, right at the bottom of the ladder. The Arabs are M2 or M3. The Spaniards, Portuguese, and other European immigrants are usually OS1. The French are automatically OS2. And you become OS3 just because of the way you look, depending on how the bosses want it. That's why I'm a skilled worker and Mouloud's a laborer, that's why I earn a few centimes an hour more, although I'm incapable of doing his work. And later they will draw up subtle statistics about the "classification grid", as the specialists say.

That's it. Mouloud has just finished his last car. The hundred and forty-eighth of the day. It's a quarter to six. The line stops. So does the noise. "So long," says Mouloud, "see you tomorrow ... Don't worry now, it'll go better." He hurries off to the cloakroom. I remain for a moment in the shop, which is emptying, my head's throbbing, my legs are unsteady. When I get to the stairs, and I'm really the last, there's no one in sight any more. The lights are out and the car bodies are motionless dark masses, waiting for the dawn and a new day's work.

I come home, exhausted and anxious. Why are all my limbs so painful? Why does my shoulder ache, and my thighs? Yet the blowtorch and the stick weren't all that heavy to carry ... It's no doubt due to the repetition of the same movement over and over again. And the tension needed to control my clumsiness. And it's because I've been standing all that time: ten hours. But the others do it as well. Are they as exhausted as I am?

I think: it's the intellectual's ineptitude for physical effort. That's naïve. It isn't just a question of physical effort. The first day in a factory terrifies everyone, many people will speak to me about it later, often with anguish. What mind, what body can accept this form of slavery, this destructive rhythm of the assembly line, without some show of resistance? It's against nature. The aggressive wear and tear of the assembly line is experienced violently by everyone, city workers and peasants, intellectual and manual workers, immigrants and Frenchman. And it's not unusual to see a new recruit give up after his first day, driven mad by the noise, the sparks, the inhuman pressure of speed, the harshness of endlessly repetitive work, the authoritarianism of the bosses and the severity of the orders, the dreary prison-like atmosphere which makes the shop so frigid. Months and years in there? How can one imagine such a thing? No: better escape, poverty, the insecurity of little odd jobs, anything!

And what about me, someone from the establishment, am I going to be able to cope? What will happen tomorrow if I still can't do that soldering? Will they throw me out? How ridiculous! A day and a half on the job ... and then fired for being incapable! And what about the others, those who haven't any diplomas and who are neither strong nor good with their hands, how will they manage to earn their living?

Night. I can't sleep. As soon as I close my eyes I see piles of 2 CVs, a sinister procession of gray car bodies. I see again Sadok's porn magazine among the sandwiches and the oil drums and the metal. Everything's ugly. And those 2 CVs, that interminable string of 2 CVs ... The alarm clock goes off. Six o'clock already? I ache all over, I'm just as worn out as I was last evening. What have I done with my night?

2

The lights of the main assembly line

I needn't have worried about it. There's no question of firing me. Two arms at four francs an hour will be very useful to Citroën, even if they're nothing special. No good at soldering? That doesn't matter, there are so many other equivalent jobs, so many nuts to tighten, so many objects to transport! If I were a black or an Arab I certainly wouldn't have the right to a second chance: they'd give me a broom, or I'd be pushing overloaded dollies. But I'm French. Even as a semiskilled worker, even as a clumsy one, I should be able to do better than wield a broom.

At seven o'clock in the morning, when the line started to move, Mouloud gave me another trial. By half past seven he had definitely given up.

"It doesn't matter, they're sure to find you something else to do. And then, you'll probably be better off. This isn't a good job, you know. Soldering makes you ill. Once a month they give me a blood test. The fellow before me, they took him off the job because he began to get sick. But they wouldn't admit that he had an industrial disease, oh no! They put him somewhere else, that's all. They'll never admit that soldering causes an industrial disease. But then, why the blood tests? ... And they'll move me from the job when I start to spit bits of metal. Don't worry, you won't be losing much."

About eight o'clock the foreman Gravier appears. "Well, Mouloud, is he all right?" Gravier is tall and solid, a good-looking type with a trace of vulgarity in his voice which indicates that he was once a worker. He's tough and the

men fear him. "Is he all right? Can he manage the job on
his own?"—"Er ... not yet, boss, I don't know if he'll be
able to." Mouloud is embarrassed, he doesn't want to do
me any harm. "He does his best, boss," he adds, for what
it's worth, "It's not easy at first ..." Gravier cuts him short
and settles the matter: "O.K., drop it." Then he turns to
me: "Come on, follow me."

Staircase. Corridors cluttered with containers. Terrifying
racket from the presses.

Staircases. Detours. Gusts of cold air. Gusts of hot air.
Fork lifts. Crowded rooms. Staircase. Then a room which
seems vast, exploding with loud noises and strident colors.
Work stations everywhere, an interminable assembly line
which runs along the longest side of a huge rectangle, and
other, smaller lines, perpendicular, transverse or oblique,
and small groups of people occupied with interior fittings,
making holes, cutting, screwing. Things moving in all
directions: on the floor, at normal height, on the ceiling.
And the procession of colored, shining, bright cars. These
colors strike me: it's a shock after the grayness of the unclad
metal in the soldering shop. And the sounds too, much
more varied and discordant. A shock, yes, but not a
pleasant one: this artificial light and this different kind of
uproar are just as hard to tolerate as the gliding metal and
the regular repetition of sounds in Gravier's area. There
was only metal there. Here it's different: it's a finishing
shop, where the cars arrive sprayed, glaring with color, here
they're "dressed", the interiors are covered, they put the
seats in, they add the headlights, the chrome, they fit the
engine into the chassis, they put in the windows and fit the
wheels. I take all that in on the way. No time to have a real
look: I have to move double-time behind Gravier's dirty
white coat. We go into an office, a big glass cage, in the
center. Another foreman sits behind a table: he's small,
plump, half-bald. Gravier introduces me with a couple of
words and dashes off. "Wait there," says the other man.
And he's deep in his papers again. They all address their
workers as *tu*, the familiar style. Why? Why this curt tone of

voice? Authority demands it. It's the system. It's one little bit of the Citroën system. Like ignoring you as you go by, like the clipped orders, like saying to someone else, in your presence, "put him at that post, there." The endless ways of telling you at every moment of the day that you don't count. Less than a spare part for a car, less than a hook from the chain (they pay attention to all those). You don't count.

I wait, standing—nobody has told me to sit down; a worker sitting down during working hours, just imagine it, that would be the end; they already tolerate the fact that he's doing nothing between his two jobs, which will earn him five or ten francs' pay for nothing, you can't imagine that on top of that they'll let him sit down! I wait without saying anything and without moving. I'm embarrassed all the same at my failure with the soldering. I don't want to be noticed.

The foreman is busy with his papers. This is Huguet, a very neat-looking gentleman, very much the businessman with a tie and a jacket underneath the freshly ironed white coat. Huguet is not just anybody: he lords it over number 85, the big assembly line, the biggest shop in the Choisy factory. He has several hundred people under him.

Right now he's showing me his balding head, which is pink and shiny. He wants to look important. He's doing something important. Checking the attendance. The work force is important. Knowing who's there and who isn't there. Who got to the time clock ten minutes late. Or even two minutes late. Oh yes! Two minutes late. You can get out of breath, put on your work clothes at high speed, cross the cloakroom with the speed of an arrow, reach your station, panting, at the very moment when the line starts to move, begin your work at exactly the same time as the others, but your punchcard has already been removed by the doorman, it ends up with the section manager and then with the foreman. Those two minutes cannot be forgotten. Got to explain yourself, my friend. And if it's the third time this month, watch out, you've lost your bonus, if you aren't thrown out. And you say: two minutes, two little minutes! and I started at the same time as the others, Citroën hasn't lost one second because of me, not the thousandth part of a 2 CV, not a centime, then why must I lose my bonus, why? And what about discipline? What are you doing to discipline? And what's the use of a foreman if his first and absolute priority isn't to see that discipline is respected? And that's why your name is now in front of Huguet who wrinkles his brow and goes through his papers with a severe expression: "Gonçalves, Antonio ... Gonçalves, Antonio ... hasn't he been late once already this month?!" That's important, knowing if you have to give a warning to someone for being late twice without an excuse. Or if you have to punish him for being late the third time. And you have to know if you can fire someone for not having sent in a medical certificate on time. These things are really important! And then, you have to see how many cars have been made during the first hour (how splendid if you've managed to do one more than the day before!). And check that the supplies ordered yesterday have arrived. And see if the problem about the stock of engines has been sorted out. And give the organization and methods office the report about the time check in the upholstery shop. All that's important, a foreman's important. Not surprising that he hasn't got one minute for me. *I*'m not in a hurry.

I wait.

No doubt there's a break in all these important activities. The white coat suddenly gives up a few seconds to concern himself with my small existence. Just at that moment a blue coat comes for information. The white coat calls out to him: "Oh, Dupré, here's a new chap. Try to put him on the door work, since you're short a person. And then don't forget to send me the list of the main paint retouching work for yesterday, I'm seeing Haulin soon." And, after these important words, which were respectfully received, the bald head bends over the papers again. A foreman is definitely a very important person. "Certainly, Monsieur Huguet," replies the blue coated Dupré, with deference. And a curt word in my direction: "Follow me."

We go out again.

Dupré is section manager and he's in a hurry. He hands me over to an adjustor. This game is all part of the hierarchy. "Show him the windshields," says the blue coat to the adjustor. "Follow me," says the adjustor. The adjustor is a very minor boss, the least important, just above the worker-craftsman. He's called that because he's supposed to "adjust" the machines; in fact, he stands around and sometimes he replaces someone at a work station, if there's some hold-up or a temporary absence. He doesn't wear a coat—which distinguishes him from the bosses—but he spends a large part of his time walking around doing nothing—which puts him in the same bracket.

This adjustor has drawn features, like a sailor after a long career at sea. He's got very red hair and I think there's an Irish look about him. He gazes at everything with the cynical expression of an adventurer who's landed by accident in this remote corner of car production. And the prospect of showing me what has to be done with the windows appears to bore him greatly. We drag ourselves to the spot. In fact it looks as though he doesn't give a damn. This is what people will say to me about him later: "He doesn't give a damn." Which, coming from workers talking about an adjustor, is certainly praise.

We arrive: a small table beside the line carrying doors which the laborers finish, adding windows, locks, chrome rims ... On the table there's a pile of windows: one of the workers from the line takes one every time a door goes past and immediately fixes the window to the moving door. My work will consist of preparing the windows, that is to say, fitting them into a rubber gasket. You do the work standing still, but obviously the speed depends on that of the line you're supplying. I've got a kind of powder, like talc, to prevent the rubber from slipping. I've got a mallet. You have to aim accurately so that the shape of the rubber fits the window exactly: if you don't get it right the first time it becomes creased or stretched, the rubber comes off at the curved parts, and you have to do it all over again. The red-haired man does two windows as a demonstration, asks me if I've understood ("Yes"), informs me in a grumbling voice that the work is piece-work and that I have to do at least three hundred and twenty windows a day. After which he strolls off, without even watching me attack my first window. Not curious.

It's immediately unpleasant, the contact of the powder and the rubber against my fingers, and the stale smell as well. I calculate: three hundred and twenty windows a day, that means thirty-two windows an hour, rather less than two minutes for each one. How many times a month, this minute little job that's offered to me for an infinite length of time? Hey, no time to think. It's urgent: the stock of windows is going down visibly, and the worker from the line who comes to take them looks at me anxiously. I start.

After half an hour I'm convinced: I've no more of a future in the finishing of windows than in soldering. Never would I have imagined that there could be so many problems in a piece of rubber, a pane of "safety" glass and white powder—with which I've quickly covered the table, the panes of glass, my jacket, and my face. Out of three windows I spoil two, and through having to do them again I've only finished six in half an hour, instead of the sixteen which constitute the minimum. And the reserve stock is almost used up. As I anxiously wipe my forehead, some unexpected help arrives.

A tall chap with a playboy air, wearing jeans and a turtleneck pullover, who was working on the doors on the line, whistling as he did so, a few yards away from my table, has left his station and without saying a word begins to do my windows. In ten minutes he completes six or seven.

The 8:15 break. I thank him. "It's nothing, it's nothing!" I'm surprised that he's been able to leave his place at the line for ten minutes. He laughs. "But Pavel and Stepan are there!" Explanation: they are three Yugoslavs who occupy three successive posts in a group which assembles complete locks—tricky work with lots of little screws to fix in difficult places. But they're so skilful and work so fast that they succeed in reducing the three jobs to two: in this way one of them in turn is always free, he can go and have a quiet smoke in the toilet or chat with the girls in the upholstery shop. It's thanks to this system that Georges—that's his name—has been able to help me out. And the boss shuts his eyes to this arrangement by the three Yugoslavs, this little team providing spontaneous mutual aid, because there's never any trouble on this part of the door assembly line (the "door roundabout", as they say). Obviously the management must have toyed with the idea of eliminating one of the three posts, since the Yugoslavs succeed in reducing them to two. But you only have to watch them work to see that no normal person could keep up such a rhythm. You might be watching sleight of hand.

I soon see that Georges enjoys the status of gang leader. Not only in the little group at this "roundabout" but in the Yugoslav community in the factory. It's a big one. Citroën concentrates nationalities in each factory. Yugoslavs at Choisy, Turks at Javel ... They take in whole groups so that they can all be put together, checked up on and spied on: house interpreters are stationed about the place, supervision at the factory and at home are combined, the fearsome political police are allowed access, Spanish and Moroccan cops, informers from the Portuguese PIDE.* The Turks come to Javel by entire villages, bringing their feudal hierarchy with them intact. Feudalism is a fine thing for Citroën! The village headman comes to the works in the morning, leading his group of twenty or twenty-five men; they carry his briefcase for him; he won't touch a tool the entire day. On paper he's a semiskilled worker like the others, but in fact he will do no more than supervise, with the blessing of Citroën. And the other Turks pay him a further commission out of their wages. Giddy whirlwind of nations, cultures, and societies, all destroyed, broken open,

* Secret police.

and ravaged, which poverty and the worldwide extension of capitalism throws, like a few crumbs, into the endless drainage canals of the work force. My comrades are from Turkey, Yugoslavia, Algeria, Morocco, Spain, Portugal, and Senegal. I've learned only snatches of their history. Who can ever recount all of it, this long march which has drawn you one by one into the jobs of semiskilled workers or laborers, the servants of the multinationals which have come to skim off the poverty of the most remote villages, and of the bureaucrats and traffickers in all kinds of permits, the ferrymen and the dealers in documents, with overloaded boats, swaying trucks, mountain passes crossed in the chilly dawn and the anguish of frontiers, and of the slavetraders and the tricksters?

Citroën has imported you, remnants torn alive from different societies, and they believe that they can control you better by leaving you like this in coagulated groups. Sometimes it's true. But what you preserve in the way of national organization is also, for you, a means of resistance, a way of existence when everything rejects you. Certain immigrants exercise over their comrades an authority which is far from duplicating the multiform authority of the management; it works in opposition and counterbalances it. Spontaneous authority of a stronger personality which respects the management, or a point of cultural resistance established by some literate man on the assembly line (can one imagine the importance for the group of the "public letter writer", who, at home, after his ten hours' work on the line, can still find the energy to write letters for his illiterate comrades?), or the legacy of past struggles (the Algerian FLN* has left various habits). I shall never know why, but for the Yugoslavs Georges is someone important. He shows it, discreetly. He smokes English cigarettes, speaks in an easy manner, and moves about between the sections of the line, the fork lifts, the containers, and the car bodies as though he were circulating among groups of

. * Liberation army.

guests in a drawing-room. His elegance is like a challenge to the Citroën machine, to the degradation of working on the assembly line. He smiles as he gives me some advice about a more rational way of handling my rubbishy collection of glass and rubber.

End of the break. Georges returns to his place and encourages me with a wink. I start again. I'm still as bad as ever. About nine o'clock the Irish-sailor adjustor comes by again, looks with a jaundiced eye at my miserable stock, and watches me struggling with an obstinate piece of rubber. "Not like that, now look ..." He does three windows again. Watches me do one. Which I make a mess of. Shrugs his shoulders, looks up at the ceiling, and goes off with an air of profound boredom. At ten o'clock I've only got one window in stock and Georges comes to the rescue just before the supply for the assembly line breaks down. Ten windows ahead. With the ones I'll succeed in doing, I'm saved ... for an hour. And then what? I really can't go through all the jobs in the works! I'm overwhelmed with anxiety again: this time they're going to fire me, surely. It's really too silly. Gloomy notions about the feebleness of the intellectuals, Hegel's dialectic about the master and the slave, atrophy of manual capacity among the part of the species who've kept pens and desks for themselves ... Talc everywhere, slippery windows, filthy rubber.

The red-haired adjustor's navigation returns him to my waters once or twice: each time he comes he completes, without a word, but with visible reproof, three or four demonstration windows. Georges comes back several times to make a new stock for me, when I'm desperate. In this way I drag along without a major catastrophe, although I'm always pursued by the speed of the door "roundabout" until noon, when shop 85 goes to eat. Temporary respite, but I've no illusions: I'm incapable of doing the job.

Canteen.

At a quarter to one we start again.

After a few seconds spent mishandling my first window of the afternoon, the red-haired fellow returns. With Dupré, the blue coat, at his side. They complement each other very well: the adjustor always looks disgusted, the section manager always looks worried.

"He won't make it," says the adjustor to the manager.

"You'll just have to put him on the seats, since Fernandez still hasn't come back," says the manager to the adjustor.

It's done: "Drop it and follow me." I put down the mallet, the talc, the Saint-Gobain glass, and the black rubber gloves, and I'm not sorry. A short walk across the shop. Each turn reveals new little corners, new areas of activity. Motionless work stations, busy work stations. Glances noticed as we go by. Boredom. Fatigue. Repetition. Anxiety. Nervous glances. Exhausted glances. A tense Black. A worn-out woman. Movement of glistening cars. Red, blue, green ...

Arrival at the upholstery shop.

Three people—one woman, two men—are standing in front of racks. They're constructing front seats for the 2 CV. On the rack you put the metal armature (the skeleton of a chair, a simple gray- or beige-colored bar, which has been twisted, retwisted, and pierced with rows of holes) and you fasten onto it two rectangles of fabric, with the help of many little rubber rings. Each ring is fitted with two symmetrical metal hooks: you place one in a hole on the metal armature, you stretch the rubber and stick the other hook into the cloth by pressing it with your thumb (you have to press in order to get through the fabric, in which there's no opening). When all the rubber rings are in position that makes a springy backrest and seat.

Next to the three racks which are in use there's a fourth one, empty: it's for me. This is piece-work again. You have to make at least seventy-five seats a day. As there are four of us, that means three hundred front seats each day, enough to equip a hundred and fifty cars: sometimes a few more come off the lines, but the firm relies on our microscopic bonus payment to force us to make up the difference, and more. Making a seat means fitting fifty hooks into the fabric: you have to press with your thumb fifty times. In order to carry out my day's production I shall have to use my thumb three thousand seven hundred and fifty times. I look reflectively at the three others, who work with the rapidity of machines, and see their thumbs covered with plasters and bandages.

"Well, do you understand?" The adjustor interrupts my reflection. "Well then, get on with it, you've no time to lose." I place an armature on the rack, take a rectangle of fabric and two rubber rings. I press with my thumb, once then I press again ...

At the end of the day I'd done twenty-five seats and Dupré, the section manager, considered that for one afternoon's work it was an encouraging start. In fact two days later I reached the required daily production of seventy-five seats. This third job could be the right one.

After the first day on the seats I'd come home with my thumbs swollen and bleeding. From the next morning, like the others, I was wearing thick bandages, their surfaces shredded by the repeated rubbing against the hooks; the protection they gave—despite this totally hideous and unpleasant decomposition, the smell and the horrible feeling of the rubber mingling with the torn plaster—was on the whole sufficient to avoid the bruising of my thumbs. However, pressing with my thumb three thousand seven hundred and fifty times a day made the blood rush there, and in the evening my hand felt so heavy and swollen that it took a good hour after the working day before it was back to normal. And when I was at home I took good care to avoid any pressure on my thumb whenever I had to pick up or hold any object. The irritation from the rubber and the decomposing bandages pursued me the whole time, blunting my senses and making me feel sick at mealtimes. Nobody mentioned it, but the others were aware of it too. We sneezed more often. Red patches on my body told me that I had an allergy starting. What should I do? I got used to it and took no more notice. But the impression remained permanently in the background. I was discovering another side to factory routine: the constant exposure to the aggression of objects, all these unpleasant, irritating, dangerous contacts with materials of all kinds: sheet iron with cutting edges, dusty pieces of scrap metal, pieces of rubber, fuel oil, greasy surfaces, splinters under the skin, chemicals which damage your skin and burn your bronchial tubes. You often get used to them, but you're never immune to them. There are certainly hundreds of allergies which are never recognized. After work you clean yourself up thoroughly, in an attempt to get rid of all that. Some people use acids or detergents, they try to scour their skins and they make things worse—they even do it at the factory, when the lines have stopped moving, under the eyes of the managers, who don't care: if they want to ruin their skins, let them do so: it won't cost Citroën anything, it isn't as though they're damaging a car body. And all those dangerous products whose effects we don't know! Tin, which will surely attack Mouloud's lungs, it's not recognized! The sprayers in the paint shop suffering from benzene poisoning, not recognized! Chronic bronchitis, frequent colds, bad coughs, asthmatic attacks, difficulties in breathing: "You smoke too much", that's the diagnosis of the imperturbable plant doctor at Citroën. And cracked, ulcerated skin. And men who rub their skin and scratch. Here, on the assembly line and at the work stations which depend on it, no one's body is protected. What about my bit of rubber allergy? Just a drop in the ocean.

The days pass, unending, ten hours at a time.

I'm getting used to my job. While my hands move back and forth I look around. During the breaks I talk a bit. My rack is a very small point in the flurry of the workshop. Around me I can see the endless jobs of the upholstery shop, foam, fabrics, rubber: a lot of women; very close to us the procession of cars which have been sprayed, passing down the big assembly line—blue, green, black, oh! and a little yellow postal van—and, farther away, the arrival of the engines on an overhead cable and the fixing of the engine to the chassis. The door "roundabout" is no longer visible but I sometimes take advantage of the break to go and say hello to Georges and the Yugoslavs.

The four of us who do the front seats form a little world of our own. I observe the three others: they've all got their own methods.

The woman works at top speed. She wears slippers, she seems to form one entity with her rack, with the workshop floor; she doesn't raise her eyes from her frame, nor speak to anyone. Her features are tense, her eyes expressionless. Her appearance amazes me. At the end of the day she's nearly always done more than ninety seats.

There's a young Frenchman with long hair and worn features. We get friendly. He's a Breton, he's not well (I'll learn later: he's tubercular), and he's called Christian. He works fairly fast. But he makes it a point of honor never to do a single chair more than the normal seventy-five: he nearly always finishes half or three-quarters of an hour before the end of the day, and spends this time walking around the shop and chatting, earning a few unpleasant looks from the bosses he meets—but he's done his production, what can they say? He's furious with the woman, whom he calls "the lunatic": "If the lunatic goes on working as hard as that they'll increase the minimum number! It's because of her that we've got to do sixty-five. Before, it was sixty seats a day, and there were five of us on the job." (There's always a "before", as with sporting records: in one place they've eliminated a post, in another they've reduced the time for an operation, somewhere else they've added ten things to be done; they always find a second, a minute, or a movement that they can cut out: won't it ever stop?) "Just look at her racing along, the lunatic! So they've put us up to seventy-five and there are only four of us now. But you can't explain to her ... And what do you think she'll get out of it in her next paycheck? Not even fifty francs!" He shakes his head in despair.

The woman pushes on hard, inaccessibly locked in her mad passion to produce seats. Apparently she's been there for years. Years spent putting in a thousand hooks a day, years spent repeating those frantic thumb movements. Does she think she'll get through it like that? Or is she afraid of the bosses? What family distress is there behind this vain struggle to produce a few seats extra? When you try to talk to her she hardly answers. I shall never know.

The third worker is a Black. He keeps to an average production: three or four seats over the regulation seventy-five, just enough to show he means well, but without fanaticism. He takes care to humor the bosses but he makes certain he won't go beyond the norm. Not easy to show your independence when you're an immigrant: who would tolerate that he should imitate Christian and go walking round the shop once he's done the required number of chairs? The first section manager he met would make trouble for him. A young Frenchman, that's just possible, but a Black! I can already hear those cutting words which are repeated a hundred times over: "If you don't want to work, get back home. We don't need any layabouts here." To go slightly beyond the required figure is the best he can do to demonstrate his fellow feeling. Christian knows this and takes it in good form. In any case we can only communicate with smiles or gestures: he doesn't speak a word of French.

As for me, I just manage to do my seventy-five seats a day. Sometimes when we close I'm two or three short.

Weeks ...

The days are getting shorter, the factory sinks into the winter, like a huge ship reduced to its engineroom. When we leave in the evening it's dark. When we start again at dawn it's dark. We live only by electric light now. We have to wait until Saturday to see daylight.

November. Soon I'll have been making seats for three months. Citroën has reduced the workday to nine and a quarter hours. With the seats, as with everything else, they've taken advantage of this change to increase our output even further: seventy seats—only five seats less, in a time reduced by three-quarters of an hour. Christian is furious. He's had a sharp exchange of words with Dupré. It's a relief to go home three-quarters of an hour earlier, it's true, but they've obviously found it necessary to make up for this by a little extra exhaustion ...

A gray cold day. I feel already tired in the morning.

Thumbstroke, rubber ring fixed, thumbstroke, rubber ring fixed, thumb, rubber, thumb, rubber, one seat finished. I put another in place, an empty frame. First thumbstroke, rubber ring. A glance at the Stakhanovite woman: she's working frantically, she's beginning her fourth chair twenty minutes after the break's over. I can see her hands moving rapidly forward and backward. The repetitive movement of the two bandaged thumbs on two rubber rings: click, click, click. It makes me dizzy. The upholstery shop moves to the rhythm of those two untiring thumbs. She sees nothing, she has her eyes fixed on her frame. My hands are heavy, my thumbs painful. How does she do it, this machine-like woman? I try to follow. Second seat done, new frame and rubber rings. She's on her fifth. Fifth or sixth?

The smell of the rubber sickens me. How does she do it? And all the others, on the main assembly line? Soldering jobs. The sharp sound of the gimlet. Hammer. Engine adjusted. Another car. Another car. And the Malian over there, who just finished screwing his sixtieth connection on the engine, can he feel his arms? Thumbstroke, rubber ring. The gimlets on the line bore into my head. I've read something about girls in Hong Kong, half-blind at the age of fifteen through wearing out their eyes assembling transistors that you can buy here for next to nothing. Where do they go, all these transistors? Where do they all go, these 2 CVs? Cars, upholstery, things, useful, useless ... Everything topples over. All these objects which people produce all the time, which devour Stepan, Pavel, Sadok, Mouloud, Christian, the seat woman, and the girls in Hong Kong whom I don't know ...

"Hey, wake up old man! Aren't you well? You're quite white." Christian in front of me, his hand shaking my shoulder. His thin, pointed face. "Hey!" Anxious look. "You mustn't go on like that, you're going to pass out. You must go to the sickbay. Wait ..."

Dupré is informed and arrives in a swirl of blue coat—spotless—sums me up, from behind his spectacles. This well-ironed cleanliness which irritates us ... "Well, what is it?" Christian: "He's ill. You've got to send him to the sickbay, he nearly passed out just now." Dupré grumbles. Hesitates. He sees how far behind I am with the seats. That doesn't please him. There's still a supply in advance at the line, but it's going down: if we don't keep it going, there will be a hold-up. Dupré's worried. After all, if I'm really ill he can replace me with someone who'll make up the backlog, it won't be any worse. He makes up his mind: "All right, I'll give you a paper."

I go off with my paper. A faint smile for Christian, who's already gone back to his seat—thumbstroke, rubber ring. It's all over for me. All over for the moment. My arms dangle in euphoria and the blood retreats from my thumbs, I can feel the swelling going down. Dizziness. Thrill of doing nothing. The first moments are intoxicating.

The sickbay. The doc: "What's the matter with him?"

Everybody hates the factory doctor. They call him "the vet", "He'd give an aspirin to a corpse", Sadok told me one day when they'd sent him back from the sickbay to the soldering shop after a quarter of an hour. He'd come back pale and exhausted, complaining of stomach pains as he picked up his blowtorch: "That doctor's a bastard." Gravier, who was lurking about, had heard him complain: "Aren't you satisfied? The door's open."—"No, boss, it's all right, I didn't say a word ..." All the work force knows that the Citroën doctors get higher bonuses in proportion to the small number of people they put off work. Their production consists of systematically sending sick men back to the line.

The sickbay, which is grayish white, smells of drugs, illness, and cars. Even here I seem to meet it again, the persistent smell of iron and rubber. I mutter that I felt ill. This large pig-like man in his white coat, who's been sold to the firm with the two chevrons, turns to the nurse and prescribes his panacea: "Well, give him an aspirin and send him back to the shop." But I must really look as though I'm in a miserable state: the nurse hesitates. "Doctor," she risks saying, "he looks feverish, perhaps we could take his temperature." The professional man agrees with a shrug of his shoulders and transfers his attention to an Algerian who arrives, looking awkward, his hand covered with blood: "How did he do that, the clumsy oaf?" The worker begins to explain in an embarrassed way; he has difficulty expressing himself in French and assumes an apologetic air, like someone saying, "I'm really sorry to disturb you."

I hand the thermometer back: it says forty degrees.

"Very well," concedes the doctor, "have him sent home by ambulance. I'll give him three days off."

They prepare the papers. I'm in a daze. Miserable sickbay, smell of disinfectant, the Algerian colleague going back to the line with his bandage, the telephone—an incidence of benzene poisoning in the paint shop, denied by the doctor, who gets angry ... who with? is it a union complaint?—industrial medicine that's been bought, I feel sick again, the smell of rubber comes back to remind me ... I still feel dizzy. The ambulance. The driver who talks to me in the fog: "You're going to have a rest." A few streets. I'm home, in bed. I think hard of things that are soft, I think of silk, the scented skin of a woman, rejecting all that, the dust, the rubber, the metal, the grayness, the line, I dream of some golden skin, I immerse myself in my fever, I plunge into a fantasy of sunshine and sea, of a warm opening, panting with desire for something else between the sheets which are already drenched with sweat.

How those three days flew by! I nursed my flu and my fatigue, saw people once or twice, long restless nights, broken with sickening reminders of rubber, disturbed by faces and cars ...

And here I am again, past the time clock and the fierce cold of the courtyard, arriving with the shivering morning shadows, parkas, jackets, and overcoats brushing against each other. "Oh, you're back, hello!"—"Hello!" Five to seven: the shop's still silent, before the racket of the lines—but this silence is a threat: everything's ready, the car bodies, the gears, the machines hold their breath before the seven o'clock explosion. Everyone knows his place, his tools, the little heap of bolts, screws, parts, pieces of rubber left yesterday, the eighteen square inches of his world. You put your snack wrapped up in newspaper down in a corner, sometimes (with older Frenchmen) the gray tin dish that the wives have filled to the brim with beef and carrots. Sitting, or leaning against something, you concentrate in order to relish the two or three remaining moments of idleness which remain, which melt away and vanish ... Oh, these gaps in time which you can't do anything with, you'd like to keep them, expand them, but you already feel yourself pulled toward the approaching moment of the start and the noise!

I go to my place. Oh, there's someone there. The man who's replaced me for these last three days is already there, he's preparing his rubber rings. He's an Algerian. He's already got bandaged thumbs.

"Hello, you're working there, on the seats?"

"Yes, they put me here. Was it you, before?"

"Yes."

He smiles and shrugs his shoulders. You're so unimportant, you can't do anything, you can do everything. One semiskilled worker replaces another in a quarter of an hour. Will they leave him there? Will they put him somewhere else? At a better post? A worse one? We'll see. Mektoub. As he waits he arranges his pieces of rubber. Seven o'clock. Racket. The line starts to move. So does he.

I remain at the side. I wait. Not for long: Dupré arrives, walking quickly, his head lowered, faithful to his image as a boss overwhelmed with worries. He calls me: "Follow me." Good, that means that I'm changing my job. No doubt the Algerian who's replacing me makes more seats than I do, and it suits Dupré to be ahead in the upholstery shop.

"You're going to unload the overhead gantries." Dupré explains it to me. The sprayed 2 CV car bodies arrive directly on the main assembly line, but incomplete. All the separate sections (doors, hoods, fenders, trunks) come from the paint shop to the main assembly line on a kind of overhead line, suspended from special hooks (the *balancelles*). My job is where the overhead line stops: I have to unhook each section as it arrives, check that there's no fault in the paint work (streaks, "tears", or running), and place it on the appropriate cart (one for the right fenders, another for the left fenders, a third for the hoods, etc.). I've got a piece of chalk to mark the faulty sections, which I put to one side: they'll go back for retouching. Every few minutes a worker comes to bring me a new empty cart and take a loaded one toward the corresponding assembly point: the doors go to the "roundabout", the other sections to various points on the main assembly line.

"There, do you understand?"

I say yes. Dupré watches me for a few minutes unhooking my bits of metal, which have been sprayed in all colors, makes certain that I'm capable of distinguishing a left-hand front door from a right-hand rear door and of putting a chalk ring round any defect in the paint work, and then goes off to see to his other managerial functions.

The worker in charge of the carts arrives a few seconds later, running along behind the one he's pushing.

"Hello, is it you now?"

Surprise: it's a Frenchman, fairly elderly. These laboring jobs are usually held by immigrants. The man has a broad, open forehead and his hair's nearly white: I think he looks like a teacher from a primary or secondary school. He wears a worn old blue boiler suit. He's quick, going rapidly from one cart to another, looking around sharply. No time to start a conversation, he's already dashed off with his load of car hoods.

Working on the gantry crane is quite a good job: you're something of a storekeeper, an inspector. Obviously you have to raise your arms a lot, but the parts aren't too heavy (the hoods more so than the others, and in particular they're awkward). And since they've been sprayed, contact with them is less unpleasant than with crude metal: there's no risk of getting a piece of steel in your fingers (in Gravier's area, the soldering shop, some pieces of metal are real moving guillotines and people cut themselves badly time after time). The difficulty is that this job is linked to others: the speed of my movements depends strictly on the mechanical system which drives the gantry crane around. When I was on piece-work I'd devised a piece of minor personal strategy in order to cheat time: I would go faster or slower, make a more intensive effort in the morning when I started, go more quietly before and after meals; I would go in for bursts of speed to break the monotony. Although it was hard working on the seats, I'd gotten used to the relative independence of the workman alone in front of his work place. "O.K., I'll do one or two more and then I'll give myself a cigarette and stop for a minute." Here that's no longer possible: the speed of the line dictates everything, without respite. At first this destruction of my remaining freedom gets me down. Then I become used to it and find an advantage in the slightest degree of fatigue I feel and in the automatic work of the unhooking. The mechanism of habit brings back a small amount of liberty: I look around, I observe life from my workshop corner, I escape in imagination, leaving just one small corner of my mind on the lookout for defects in spraying.

Unloading the gantry cranes. New routine.

The cranes are near the door "roundabout". So here I am once more a few yards from the three Yugoslavs, quite near my short-lived post in window-preparing. This coming and going has expanded my world. A whole section of the workshop is familiar to me now: from upholstery to the cranes, by way of the start of the big assembly line and the door "roundabout".

The clattering network which had left me dazed the first time I met it has gradually fallen into place, after the itineraries, encounters, and the posts I occupied. The containers still pile up, the fork lifts still rush about, there are still the right angles and the sharp recesses along the glass-walled offices of the charge hand and the section manager, but I've worked out a routine: visits to the door roundabout to say hello to the Yugoslavs; the third step of the staircase which goes up to the paint shop, adopted now as the usual place for our snack; now it's Christian, who comes to chat during the breaks or at the end of the day. A few trails blazed, a few familiar faces: enough to mark out a universe. Enough to embed yourself in the slow, uneventful passing of the nine and a quarter hours of the working day. Enough for the days to pass—slowly, so slowly! —indistinguishable, interchangeable: was it Tuesday or Wednesday, then, that Dupré lost his temper with the Malian in the chassis assembly area? Was it a week ago that Sadok came to see me at the three o'clock break, or was it already two weeks ago?

It's like a gradual anesthesia: you could curl up in the torpor of nothingness and watch the months go by—years, perhaps, why not? With always the same exchanges of words, the customary gestures, the wait for the morning break, then the wait for five o'clock in the evening. From engine-check to engine-check the day always comes to an end. When you've survived the shock of starting, the real danger is there. Numbness. Forgetting even the reasons for one's own presence here. Being satisfied with this miracle: surviving. Getting used to it. You get used to everything, apparently. Letting yourself melt into the mass. Softening the blows. Avoiding incidents, being on your guard against everything that disturbs you. Negotiating with one's fatigue. Seeking refuge in a sub-life. Temptation ...

You concentrate on little things. A minute detail

occupies a whole morning. Will there be fish in the canteen? Or chicken in sauce? Before coming to the factory I had never understood with such clarity the meaning of the word "economy". Economy of movements. Economy of words. Economy of desires. This intimate part of the finite quantity of energy which everyone carries within himself, which the factory draws out of him, must be measured out now if you want to retain a minute fraction of it, and not be left completely drained. Yes, at the three o'clock break I'll go and give a newspaper to Sadok and discuss what's happening in Gravier's area. And yet no. I'm too tired today. I have to go down a flight of steps, up another one, and then rush back. Another day. Or when we go home. This afternoon I don't feel capable of taking any time off my ten minutes' break. Others, who are sitting down around me, with empty expressions on their faces, are making the same calculations: should they go to the end of the workshop to talk to so-and-so or borrow a cigarette from him? Or get some lemonade from the vending machine on the second floor? They're thinking about it. Economy. Citroën measures out to the very second the actions they extort from us. We measure our fatigue down to each movement.

How could I have imagined that they could have stolen one minute from me, and that this theft would cause me more pain and hurt than the most sordid of crimes? When the line starts up again with brutal treachery after only nine minutes of break there are loud yells from every corner of the shop: "Hey, it's not time! One more minute! ... Bastards!" Shouts, pieces of rubber being thrown about, conversations interrupted, groups of men dispersing rapidly. But the minute's been stolen, everyone starts again, nobody wants to slip back or get behind, to be in trouble for half an hour trying to recover his normal position. But we miss that minute. It hurts us. The word that's been interrupted feels the hurt. The unfinished sandwich feels the hurt. The question that remains unanswered feels the hurt. One minute. They've stolen one minute from us. It's precisely that minute which would have allowed us a rest, and it's lost forever. Sometimes, in fact, this trick doesn't work: too much fatigue, too much humiliation. They won't have that minute, we won't let it be stolen from us: instead of subsiding, the angry noise swells, the whole shop echoes with it. The shouting gets louder and louder and three or four bold workers finally rush up to the start of the line, switch off the current and make it stop again. The bosses come running, get angry because they feel they must, and brandish their watches. During this discussion the minute we're arguing about has quietly gone by. This time it's we who've won! The line starts up again without anyone saying a word. We've defended the break time, we feel so much more rested! Minor victory. There are even people smiling along the line.

These frays wake you up, they put you on your guard. And then the drowsiness of repeated actions comes over you again. Oh, let's snuggle down in our routine, save our strength, accept the anesthesia, avoid everything that upsets and exhausts us a little further ... One Prussian-blue fender, one white hood, one left-hand back door—streaked, I mark it. Take no notice of anything. Break: relish it. A cigarette. Exchange a few harmless words with the cart man. Not too many. Don't exhaust yourself. Start again. Soon lunch time. Think about the menu. One fender. One hood. One door.

The calm of nothingness? Impossible. The overhead gantry isn't an island. The world comes to blow up a storm.

The cart man had intrigued me since the first day I saw him. Why was a fairly elderly Frenchman a laborer? Strange, this teacher's head emerging from a blue smock that's too big, threadbare, like some prison uniform. He was always on the move, fairly talkative and apparently always anxious, he would talk about this and that during the few moments when his trips across the shop brought him over to stock up some parts arriving on the overhead gantry. He had introduced himself: Simon.

One morning Simon comes to see me during the break. He looks upset. During the first hour and a quarter of work, in contrast to his usual behavior, he hasn't said a word, rushing along behind his carts even faster than usual. During the break he asks me very quickly, in an embarrassed way: "Can you lend me two hundred francs? My wife's ill. Pleurisy. We're absolutely broke. It's for medicines."

I've got this sum on me: I give it to him.

He's relieved. We start to talk. I ask him why he's a laborer, and if he can't get a better paid job with Citroën.

He hesitates before replying. Then he rolls his eyes in fright.

"Listen, they've already shut their eyes in taking me on, I can't complain, I have to be careful."

He hesitates again. I say nothing, I'm intrigued. He goes on in a subdued voice:

"The fact is, I've got a record. A police record."

Simon? A police record? This quiet old man? He tells me the story. His wife, constantly ill (lungs), the doctor's bills, the drugs. He couldn't pay his rent any more. Sheriff, foreclosure on his goods, finally he's thrown out. He finds himself in the street, with his wife. In the rush some personal effects (especially clothes) remained inside. It's winter. They must be gotten out, at once. He breaks the seals that have been placed on the door to his apartment and takes out his bits of things. For this crime (violation of domicile), he was brought before a court which sentences him to three years' imprisonment with suspended sentence. THREE YEARS.

And since then he's had a "record", lives in permanent fear, and contents himself with the worst paid jobs, he plays it quiet and is only too pleased that people "shut their eyes".

They're doing him a favor, aren't they? For, in principle, Citroën demands a clean record from its work people: you have to show it during the two weeks after you're taken on, before the end of the trial period. It's obvious that before you can work on the assembly line it's essential to show genuine proof of good conduct. They're not going to pay eight hundred francs a month for ten hours' work a day to crooks! But once this rigorous selection has been made, don't imagine that Citroën considers its workers to be honest people. No. For Citroën, all workers are potential thieves, delinquents who haven't yet been found out. We're the object of rigorous supervision by the guards, who frequently carry out searches as we leave the factory for home ("Hey, you there! ... Yes, open your bag ..." "Let's see inside your overcoat, it looks full of something."). Humiliating, hesitant, stupid searches. Sandwiches carefully unwrapped. For the workers, obviously. No one will ever search one of the cars in which the senior staff drive around freely: everyone knows that they take away whole gear boxes and help themselves freely to accessories. For them, impunity is assured. But the poor fellow who's been picked up for taking a screwdriver will certainly be fired on the spot.

Simon's story has chilled me. I can't get over his three years, his record. He seems relieved by having told me his secret. Now we're accomplices. He tells me in bits the story of his life and keeps me up-to-date with the progress of his wife's illness. And between two carts full of doors and hoods, he suddenly confides to me his sadness at having had no children, and his worry about being alone if anything were to happen to his wife.

I talk to him a little about myself as well. A kind of trust is set up between us. His confidences gradually make me see him in a different light. He gives the impression of being obedient, but he's still rebellious. He's only concealing that part of him. He has the sly tricks of a schoolboy. He confides to me his secret participation in attempted strikes, little acts of sabotage, the passing of leaflets from hand to hand. He tells me with excitement about incidents at the Citroën-Choisy works in May 1968, when Junot, the hated section manager, was locked out, his effigy hanged outside the main entrance, the works occupied and barricaded.

Simon stayed there day and night, doing small jobs for the pals on the strike picket, helping to fortify the works, and setting up traps in case there was an attack by the CRS,* and yet taking care that he wasn't too much noticed from the outside. Always "on the quiet" ("I have to be especially careful, you understand").

Among his carts he dreams aloud about the revolution and his eyes sparkle as he talks to me. But as soon as one of the bosses appears he lowers his head, assumes once again the expression of an honest, anxious worker, and busies himself carting off his car hoods and fenders to the other end of the workshop.

Around the main assembly line there's a complex social life, exacerbated by the presence of many women in the upholstery shop. Christian, who's inquisitive, always has an opinion about each of them. One afternoon he comes to see me during the break. The Yugoslavs are there too, Georges with his eternal cigarette between his lips. A few yards farther on a blonde woman, with heavy make-up and her hair in a ponytail, is deep in conversation with Dupré, the charge hand. He is obviously in the process of trying to date her, and the woman, leaning against his work table and smiling, isn't discouraging him. Christian gives them an unpleasant look, spits on the floor and hisses between his teeth: "The cow! She goes out with the bosses!" It came out very quickly, with all the vivacity you expect from a Breton. Georges, who seemed absentminded and was looking elsewhere, reacted at once, and, looking Christian in the eyes, said: "Why do you say that? She's doing no harm to anyone. Life's not easy for a woman on her own, she does the best she can. The bosses who take advantage of it are the buggers. Not her." There was a silence. Everyone was trying to think of a new subject of conversation when the end of the break separated us.

A few days later I was going out of the factory with

* Riot police.

Christian, by chance, and we passed the same woman in the street. She had a little boy with her, and was holding his hand very tightly. The child looked radiant, and he was well dressed. She walked firmly ahead, gazing at him, untouched by the din of the traffic, aware only of her pride as a mother. No sign any more of the coquette from shop 85 whom we'd seen "getting herself in good" with the boss. You only had to look at her just then to realize that everything she did was done for her little boy. Christian looked at me shamefacedly and said nothing. I never heard him criticize the behavior of the workshop women again.

My work as an inspector leads me to meditate: checking the perfect condition of these smooth car bodies, what nonsense! A tear mark on this left fender: put aside, back to the paint shop! Irregularity on this polish: back for retouching! The paint has run slightly at the edge of this white hood: to be done again! Check. Recheck. It must shine, it must appear perfect, it must hit the buyer between the eyes. For, after all this, there's the selling. Through this dictatorship of the object (the least imperfection directs the attention of the hierarchy upon you), there's the dictatorship of the sales department over us: salesmen, representatives, agents, publicity men, those who oil the wheels of marketing, themselves subject to the whims of fashion, outward appearance, and status. They're not selling cars, they're selling glittering dreams. And if you know that after a few days' use the car will in any case have lost its marvelous perfection it doesn't matter: what counts is that it dazzles you in the showroom. And there we are like idiots, inspecting, touching, retouching, smoothing, supervising. Supervising? But it's we who are supervised, supervised by these smooth surfaces, always identical and begun all over again: sky blue, midnight blue, vermilion, emerald. A streak or an inadequate coat of paint give us away, and if there are too many faults, there's an uproar among the bosses, white coats come running along, even three-piece suits. At that point it's serious: a senior person doesn't put himself out for nothing. You have to see them in their agitation, the people from "O and M" or from "Sales", testing out the material, calculating the imperfections of the varnish or the chemical coating, wondering if it's not too hot, too cold, too damp—for the car, of course! As for us, we can die of heat or shiver in cold draughts, they don't give a damn. They don't see us, they push us out of the way with a gesture of impatience if we hamper their movements, if by some unfortunate chance we get in the light. Sometimes the charge hand rushes up in a servile fashion and makes explicit the impatient gesture by the man in the suit: "Now, get out of the way, old man, you can see you're in Monsieur Bineau's way!" while the Bineau in question contemplates the piece of sprayed scrap iron with the gestures of an art lover, standing back, coming close, narrowing his eyes, standing in the light, while the others hold their breath in order not to disturb the expert evaluation.

The car bodies, the fenders, doors, and hoods are smooth, shining, multicolored. We, the workers, are gray, dirty, crumpled. Color has been drawn off by the object: there's none left for us. The car under production glows with all its fire. It comes forward gently, moving through the stages of its fitting, enriched with accessories and chrome, its interior is embellished with soft fabrics, all attention is on the car. It laughs at us. It scorns us. For it, and it alone, shine the lights of the main assembly line. As for us, we're enveloped in invisible darkness.

How can one fail to be overwhelmed with a desire to destroy? Who among us doesn't dream now and then of taking revenge on these blasted insolent cars, so tranquil, so smooth—so smooth!

Occasionally some people crack up and go into action. Christian tells me the story of a guy who actually did it here, in shop 85, shortly before I came—everyone still remembers it.

He was a Black, a tall hefty fellow, who spoke French with difficulty, but he spoke a little all the same. He was fixing parts of a dashboard into place with a screwdriver. Five screws to fix on each car. That Friday afternoon he must have been on his five hundredth screw of the day. All at once he began to yell and rushed at the fenders of the cars brandishing his screwdriver like a dagger. He lacerated a good ten or so car bodies before a troop of white and blue coats rushed up and overcame him, dragging him, panting and gesticulating, to the sickbay.

"And what happened to him then?"

"They gave him an injection and he was taken to the mental hospital by ambulance."

"Didn't he ever come back?"

"Yes, he did. They kept him at the hospital for three weeks. Then they sent him home saying it wasn't serious, just a mental depression. Then Citroën took him back."

"On the assembly line?"

"No, on piece-work, close by his old job: yes, they put him to sheathing cables over there, where that Portuguese is now. I don't know what they did to him in the hospital, but he was odd. He always seemed absentminded, he never said a word to anyone any more. He sheathed his cables, looking into space, saying nothing, he hardly moved ... He was as still as a stone, you know. Cured, so-called. And then one day he was never seen again. I don't know what happened to him."

3

The shop floor committee

December on the cranes ...

There are moments of exasperation. What have I done, over four months, beyond making 2 CVs? I didn't join Citroën to make cars, but "to organize the working class". A contribution to the resistance, to the struggles, to the revolution. In our student debates I was always opposed to those who thought of "the establishment" as an experiment in individual reform: for me, the employment of intellectuals has no meaning outside the political one. And now, here, it's this very political effectiveness itself which escapes me. Where can I start? A factory's a huge place. Even if there are only twelve hundred people here. You can't know everyone. You meet people by chance, friendships form. The man on the job next to yours. A friendly chap who starts to talk to you in the canteen. The cloakroom. All this allows you to carry on, it gives you a bit of fresh air. But it's chance, and that does not necessarily put you in touch with the most "militant" people, as they call them.

Seen from outside the business of getting into "the establishment", into the movement, seems obvious: you get taken on and you organize. But here this entry "into the working class" disintegrates into a vast number of small individual situations among which I can't find a solid footing. These very words, "the working class", don't have the same immediate meaning to me as they had in the past. Not that I've come to doubt that they embrace a profound reality, but the variety and mobility of this semiskilled population into which I've been thrown have upset me, submerged me. Everyone here is a case. Everyone has his story. Everyone chews over his tactics and in his own way tries to find a way out. How can I find a direction in this semi-penitentiary, indefinitely provisional universe: who can imagine that he can "make a career" as a semiskilled worker? Who doesn't both resent deeply his presence here and see the wretchedness of his small-time bits of work as a kind of decline or accident? People dispense with scheming, they dream of going back to their own country and opening a little business. Many of them persist in betting, and only succeed in reducing still further their meager wages of four hundred francs every two weeks. Others do "jobs" outside. What "jobs"? And then there's trafficking in various things. And "moonlighting" on Saturdays and Sundays: when they do that, after a week's work on the line, there's a good risk that they'll soon kill themselves.

Yes, how can I get a foot in?

I make a list of my friends, the workers I know, the ones I could try to get together.

Christian, the tubercular Breton from the upholstery shop. He's eighteen and looks sixteen. Lively, nervous. He's still on the seats. Exasperated by the stupid way the days pass: nine and a quarter hours of thumbstrokes-rubber-seat ... As though that wasn't enough, he has endless problems with his girlfriend and her parents. He arrives in the morning with drawn features and red eyes. His girlfriend is at a *lycée* and her family don't like to see her going out with a workman. And then, since he lives in a Citroën hostel with military-style discipline, they haven't got a place where they can meet. One evening I invited them to my place and let them have a room. An odd couple. She's gentle and smiling, much taller than he is. He talks excitedly, he makes plans, she listens in fascination. Soon afterward they found a maid's bedroom, and Christian describes his weekends to me: since they have no money they stay in bed all day, knitting side by side. I imagine it. Just the knitting showing above the blankets. Christian, with the same keen eyes that he has in the workshop, counting his stitches. And plans, always plans ... It's tough coming back to the upholstery shop on Monday morning, and the song-and-dance of thumbstroke-rubber. Surely, if the occasion arises, Christian will do something. But what can I offer him? I've spoken to him about China, Vietnam. I gave him newspapers. "Not bad, your book," and then he'd talked about something else.

Sadok, the Algerian with Asiatic features whom I'd noticed "slipping back" on the first day in Gravier's section, often invites me to La Choppe, the café right beside the works. At five o'clock, after leaving the cloakroom, he waits for me, and in a hesitant voice, as though he were asking something really important, says "Will you have a beer?" And almost always he remains silent in front of his glass. He smiles vaguely. He seems glad just to have a bit of company. In the evening he hesitates over leaving the factory and his immediate surroundings. He hangs about. There's something extreme about his fear of solitude, it's almost panic. From the scraps of information he gives me I understand that he hasn't any roots, even in Algeria. The war destroyed everything. Nobody writes to him, there's no one for him to write to. If he were to have an accident it wouldn't affect anyone. He would disappear without leaving a ripple on the surface.

One day he came to see me, very upset. His landlord (a crook: three beds one above another in a tiny room) had thrown him out. He had no more money. He didn't know where he could sleep. He was afraid that if the police found him lying down somewhere in a public place they'd take him away. I put him up for several nights, until he found a place in a hostel. From then on he comes to see me every day during the break or invites me to the café. He gives me news about the soldering shop and Mouloud, the Kabylian. "It doesn't change, you know. The soldering's faster all the time. More cars all the time."

I've given him newspapers, too. But I feel he's terrified by Gravier and he's drifting somewhat.

And all the others. Simon, the Yugoslavs, my neighbors on the line, the people who sit at the same table in the canteen, old Jojo from the paint shop who has his locker in the cloakroom next to mine. Discussions, rapid exchanges, the passing of time, the brief encounters in the cloakroom, the crush in the self-service at noon, interruptions during the break. "Oh, hello! See you soon."

Sometimes I'm able to describe a strike in Brittany with occupation of the factory and lock-out. Or I tell how, in a steelworks in Shanghai, workers made huge holes in the walls so that there would be some communication with the outside world and so the place of production wouldn't look like a prison. Or I speak of education in France and the subtle way in which children of workers and peasants are eliminated. And what next?

Groping.

Scraps of propaganda.

Counting possible activists.

All this leaves me unsatisfied. It doesn't make up for the hundred and forty-five 2 CVs which go out, in their undisturbed way, every day. I'd thought of myself as an ardent agitator, here I am as a passive worker. Prisoner of my job.

Sometimes I try to analyze what makes up this net in which I'm caught.

First, there's the work. It's come down on top of me. For a long time it's been crushing everyone. Ten hours or nine and a quarter hours of tense movements, broken by short gaps during which everyone tries most of all to get his breath back. All the rest of life is brutally compressed, stunted, broken up. Conversation has to be crammed into the few minutes of the break or the rapid meal in the canteen. One morning you start a conversation with your neighbor in the cloakroom about a dangerous machine and the high number of industrial accidents at Citroën. You give figures, you describe what happens at the Javel works. That interests him a good deal, he begins to explain his ideas about what ought to be done. A few minutes have passed, work starts again and separates you, you both have to dash off to your workshop, you promise each other that you'll carry on with the talk that evening. When you get back to the cloakroom, more than ten hours have passed, everyone's tired, you've forgotten where you'd gotten to, so has he. You try all the same to pick up the discussion again, but he's in a hurry to leave, he says to you quickly: "Yes, we must talk about it again another time, so long now!" and he's already disappeared.

Time has become a scarce commodity.

Holding a meeting. Outside, it's really the easiest thing. But here, in the works, I suddenly have the feeling that it's indecent to ask my workmates for two or three hours of their time, without a serious reason, just in order to see what we could do. However, it often happens that the end of the week brings them only boredom and a melancholy countdown of the hours that precede the start of work on Monday. Some of the young ones party: they go out together, they dance or go to the movies. Or they just get drunk. But most of the workers, especially among the immigrants, enter into a type of lethargy: they walk slowly, they talk together, they stay for ages in the cafés. During this provisional collapse muscles and nerves attempt to recover their strength. For a long time now on Sunday afternoons I've seen immigrant workers in the taverns of the thirteenth arrondissement, sitting in a motionless, dreaming way in front of beers that they've hardly sipped. In the past I hardly paid them any attention. Now I do. In their expressions I recognize the anxiety about passing time, with which they can't do anything, the painful awareness of each wasted minute which brings them nearer to the roar of the assembly line and another week of exhaustion.

Then I tell myself that I must respect the way these people live, that one can't unexpectedly break through a feeling of equilibrium that has so much difficulty in reconstituting itself every evening and every weekend ...

And then, there's fear.

Difficult to define. At first I would notice it individually, in one man or another. Sadok's fear. Simon's fear. The fear of the woman working on the seat rubbers. In each case one could find an explanation. But as time passes I feel that I'm up against something bigger. Fear is part of the works, it's a vital cog in the system.

In the first place it's expressed in all this mechanism of authority, supervision, and repression that surrounds us: watchmen, foremen, charge hands, section managers. The section managers most of all. It's a Citroën specialty: a local personnel officer, just for a few workshops, an official cop, who keeps an eye on the guards, keeps up-to-date with sanctions and punishments, presides at dismissals. He wears a suit, he's got nothing whatever to do with production: his function's purely repressive. The one we have, Junot, as is often the case, is a former colonial army officer who's retired from military service and taken up work with Citroën. He's a red-faced alcoholic and treats immigrants like natives as in the good old days: with scorn and hatred. Plus, I think, a notion of revenge: they must be made to pay for the loss of the Empire. When he prowls around a shop everyone checks his post more or less and pretends to concentrate entirely on his work; conversations stop abruptly, the men fall silent, and the only noise to be heard is that of the machines. And if you're called "to the office", or the foreman signals that he wants to talk to you, or even if a guard in a cap calls out to you suddenly in the yard, your heart always sinks a little. Fine, this is all well known: inside the works you're in an accepted police state, on the brink of lawbreaking if you're found a few yards from your work station or in a corridor without a paper duly signed by a superior, in trouble for a defect in production, liable to be fired on the spot if there's a scuffle, punishable for being a few seconds late or for an impatient remark to a charge hand, and endless other things which hang over your head, which you don't even think about, but they're not forgotten by guards, foremen, section managers, and *tutti quanti*.

Fear, however, is even more than that: you can easily pass a whole day without seeing any of the bosses at all (because they're shut in their offices dozing over their papers, or because an impromptu conference has miraculously rid you of them for a few hours), and in spite of that you feel that the anxiety is still there, in the air, in the behavior of the people around you, in yourself. No doubt it's partly because everyone knows that the official system of discipline at Citroën is only the visible part of the firm's police system. We have among us informers of all nationalities, and especially the house trade union, the CFT, a collection of strikebreakers and election-riggers. This "yellow" union is cherished by the board of directors: membership makes it easier for executives to be promoted and the section manager often forces immigrants to join it, threatening them with dismissal or with expulsion from the Citroën hostels.

But even this does not entirely define our fear. It's made up of something more subtle, more profound. It's closely linked to the work itself.

The line, the procession of 2 CVs, the timed movements, this world of machines where you feel in danger of losing your foothold at every moment, of "slipping back", "missing", being overwhelmed, being rejected. Or injured. Or killed. Fear oozes out of the factory because the factory, at the most elementary, obvious level, constantly threatens the men it uses. When there's no boss in sight, and we forget the informers, it's the cars that are watching us through their measured progress, our own tools that are threatening us at the slightest inattention, the gears on the line that are calling us to order in brutal fashion. The dictatorship of the owners is exercised here in the first place by the all-powerfulness of the objects.

And when the factory's humming, when the carts rush down the corridors, when the gantry cranes drop their car bodies with a crash, when the tools scream together, and every few minutes the lines spit out a new car which is seized by the moving corridor, when all that works on its own and the accumulated din of endless operations repeated without interruption resounds permanently in our heads, we remember that we're men, and how much more fragile we are than the machines.

Terror of the grain of sand.

I've taken my CGT* card. But in this area it's all very quiet. The union branch runs the welfare committee (canteen, holiday homes, social work) and uses up most of its power doing so, all the more so since the Citroën management fights a war of attrition against it. Battles about statistics, deficits, and subsidies which are refused. From time to time a leaflet denounces the sabotage of the CE by the employers, or calls for a day's shutdown by the combined metalworkers' unions. On those days a few workers go to the cloakrooms an hour earlier than the others. They are immediately replaced and production continues as though nothing had happened. The CGT is especially strong among the craftsmen, the French workers who carry out maintenance work. It was old Jojo, my neighbor in the cloakroom, who sold me my card: he follows union affairs fairly closely, especially since he himself is engaged in a determined attempt to have his bronchial troubles recognized as an industrial disease (he's been working for years in the paint shop). But most of the workers see the union as one of the factory institutions. They talk of it this way as though it were a last resort: "One of these days I'm going to go up and see the delegate about this bonus situation..." Early in January I went to the annual meeting for the renewal of subscriptions. There were fifteen people sitting around aperitifs.

Resistance. I guess it to be concealed deep down among the groups of immigrant nationals. Whispered in Kabylian, Arabic, Serbo-Croatian, Portuguese. Disguised beneath a simulated resignation. It comes through, strong and

---

* Confédération Générale du Travail: one of the biggest trade unions; the communist union.

unexpected, in the row caused by the loss of a minute at break. It buzzes in the excitement of Fridays, when the men on the line are suffering from worn nerves, when pieces of rubber and nuts fly in all directions, and mysterious accidents often immobilize the gears. Or in a more modest way, it's expressed in a simple offer of help: the neighbor whom you prevent from slipping back by doing part of his work before he goes under; Georges, the Yugoslav, coming to my help on the windows when he knew nothing about me, except my obvious failure to cope. Attitudes, too. Holding yourself straight. Taking as much care as possible about your clothes.

From this point of view the cloakroom fascinates me. It functions like a sieve and every evening a spectacular collective metamorphosis takes place. In a quarter of an hour, in feverish agitation, each man tries to remove from his body and his outward appearance the traces of the day's work. Ritual of cleansing and restoration. They want to go out clean. Better, smart.

Water from the few washbasins runs in all directions. Scraping off the dirt, soap, powders, energetic rubbing, cosmetic products. Strange alchemy in which there are still traces of sweat, smells of oil and metal. Gradually the smells of the workshops and fatigue subside and give way to that of cleaning. At last, the men unfold and put on their clothes for outside: a perfectly clean shirt, often a tie. Yes, it's a sieve, on one side is the stagnating atmosphere of despotic production and on the other the theoretically free air of civilian society. On one side, the factory: dirt, worn jackets, overalls that are too big, stained blue boiler suits, slouching gait, the humiliation of orders to which there is no reply ("Hey, you!"). On the other, the city: suit, polished shoes, upright walk, and the hope of being called "mister".

Of all the immigrants the Blacks pay most attention. The insignificant sweeper, in his loose, shapeless, gray garment, whom I saw ten minutes ago pushing his heap of dust from step to step, comes out of the works now: finely striped suit, very white shirt, tie, gleaming shoes, attaché case. Several workers arrive and leave with attaché cases in their hands—which usually contain a sandwich for the break, sometimes a racing paper to help with betting slips. To pass in the street or the subway for an office worker, a civil servant, a responsible African on a mission ... In any other circumstances I would find this get-up ridiculous. Here, it seems to be a natural part of the resistance by the OS. Use every opportunity to show that you won't allow yourself to be submerged. Just one way of advertising your self-respect.

It's here, in these minute signs of resistance that I observe every day, more than in political analysis, that I find real reasons for hope. At the worst moments of exasperation there's still a vague, almost unconscious, certainty that there's a subterranean power quite near, and one day it will break out.

So I have to wait. I tell myself that something will happen in the end.

And something did eventually happen. In January.

Twice over. First, the meeting with Primo. Then provocation from Citroën in the form of a staff notice.

I met Primo while distributing leaflets. That morning Yves, the schoolboy who worked in conjunction with me outside the Citroën works at Choisy, was handing out a leaflet that we had duplicated the day before. It was a violent denunciation of the CFT, the "yellow" union, whose men had recently distinguished themselves again by rounding up militants outside the Javel factory.

It's still dark, and the distribution takes place in silence. As a rule the workers who are coming in take the leaflet which Yves offers them, fold it carefully, and slip it into their pockets, keeping it to read (or have it read to them) at a quiet moment during the day. Some start to read it as they walk along. Hardly anyone stops. The biting cold, the apprehension of facing another day of work, everyone's tense. Only one worker, a short man, very upright in his overcoat, paused and stood still beside Yves, reading the leaflet with concentration. When he's finished he says in a loud voice which rings out strangely in the freezing air:

"But it's true what they say there! We're not going to let those bastards tread on us without ever doing anything!"

Turning towards Yves he adds:

"Good work, comrade! You're right and you're not afraid, that's fine. You must keep it up."

And he shakes hands with the boy, keeping his arm almost tense, in a stiff, ceremonial attitude as though they were signing a treaty. Yves blushes with emotion and energetically returns this unexpected handshake. It's not a lighthearted gesture. For some time the CFT men have been regularly provoking fights whenever militant left-wing leaflets are handed out, and they try to terrorize the workers who take them. At the Javel works some men have already been seriously hurt: one man lost an eye and others were left bleeding on the pavement. Reports of this spread immediately to us at Choisy and the atmosphere worsened. For the little man in the overcoat to show his solidarity the way he did is a courageous act. Yves thanks him, brokenly. Then he undertakes to recount to him in detail the incidents at Javel, and the provocations of the CFT, and how we hope to be able to respond with the workers. The other man listens attentively. Nods approval. Asks for precise facts. Reacts violently when Yves quotes a name he knows ("Oh, I know him, Tabucci, he's a swine, he comes hanging about here too, he's always whispering with Junot!").

Three or four workers have stopped and stand in a circle to listen. I was standing a few paces away, as I always do at these distributions. I come up to the group and join in the discussion. The maneuvers of the CFT, even at the Choisy works, the immigrants whom the section manager forces to join the "yellow" union, the police spies at the works and in the hostels ... The man approves, giving examples which I didn't know about. Then, noticing the time: "Well, I must be off, or I'll be late. So long, boys, and keep it up!"

He goes into the factory, showing his card to the guard as usual. I follow him. "Hey, do you work here too? What shop are you in? So we'll meet again!" We made a date to meet in the canteen at noon, to talk.

I often see Primo now. He works in the paint shop, above us. Number 84. The shop full of poisonous vapors, damaged lungs, benzene poisoning, and blood diseases. But also the most militant shop, determined to have their industrial diseases recognized and to make Citroën modernize its unhealthy premises, which are badly ventilated and a constant fire hazard.

Primo is Sicilian. He speaks French very well but with a strong accent. Responsibilities fell on him very early in life and he faced up to them by coming here. He was the eldest of a big peasant family, the bad harvests and the unemployment of the *Mezzogiorno* made him decide to emigrate. He sends money regularly to the *famiglia*, gives his opinion by letter on the events in the village, and follows the studies of his younger brothers and sisters, to whom he addresses his advice and instruction with the greatest care.

He's not yet thirty but looks much older, with receding hair which leaves him almost bald, and the sun-baked cheeks typical of a peasant from the extreme south (his forehead is paler, due to his wearing a hat, and contrasts oddly with his brick-colored face). Only his smile, which has something childish about it, contradicts the premature aging of his features. He walks in a very upright way, always wearing dark clothes, not caring too much about them but not neglecting them, and I imagine that if you saw him in the street you'd hesitate before summing him up: something between a farmer in his Sunday best and a provincial notary.

The gray or black clothes that he wears outside the factory seem to be so much a part of him that I always have a moment's surprise when I see him in the canteen rush, wearing his paint sprayer's overalls. True, it's a spectacular get-up: a loose green tunic, rubber boots, splashes of color everywhere, even on his face. The colleagues from the paint shop look like deepsea divers and give the impression of emerging from some putrid bath, still impregnated with chemical odors which get in your throat.

These canteen conversations with Primo become a regular rendezvous. He's precise and wastes no words, he always uses these twenty minutes as completely as possible. Everything interests him. I pass on to him newspapers and books, I tell him what I know about Citroën, about other factories, about the situation in France. At the moment there are rumors about a possible merger of Citroën and Fiat, how would that work? Would Agnelli reorganize Citroën on Italian lines? Perhaps we'll be able to link our struggles with those going on in Turin, which are very intense at the moment. The unions. The transfers. Security. Primo himself has a precise knowledge of the system of exploitation that operates in the place, he knows its weak points and the state of mind among the workers. He never says, "We metalworkers", because he speaks without pompousness, but something in his manner expresses it continually. Although he has never been a factory worker in Italy he remains close to his friends in the Italian automobile industry, who, like him, often came from the south. The guerilla strikes in Piedmont—work schedules overthrown and the start of worker control of production—fascinate him. When he explains, when he asks questions, I have a strong feeling of the reality of this international proletariat to which Primo belongs and which he never forgets. Metalworkers from Citroën, Fiat, Berliet, Peugeot, Chrysler, Renault, and Ford: millions of men on the car assembly lines, controlled by similar workings, united across the frontiers in the repetition of identical movements and in a resistance to multiple production.

But Primo doesn't become entangled in abstractions. Fate has made him a worker at Citroën, and it's here that things are happening. No detail of daily oppression leaves him unmoved. As a grassroots trade unionist he has no responsibility beyond his own ideas about the dignity of the worker. That's enough to keep him constantly on the alert. He wastes no time in "going to see the delegate" to tell him about the case of a colleague in difficulty. And he very regularly gives me precise information about his workshop, to help complete our leaflets:

"In the paint shop the ventilation doesn't always work properly. Yesterday one more worker went down with health trouble. Let us demand from the management elementary health precautions ... Signed: The colleagues from shop 84."

About mid-January a brief directive from the management was displayed in every shop and warned us that in one month's time, in mid-February, "recuperation" would come into force again.

"Recuperation". A bitter word, coming like the cancellation of concessions gained in autumn 1968. During the strikes of May and June the workers had obtained a few moderate financial gains from the management, who were alarmed. Everyone had accepted them as payment for the strike days, imposed on the bosses by a link-up of forces. But Citroën did not see it like that. As soon as order was restored the management announced that they would reimburse themselves through unpaid extra work: the day's work is prolonged by forty-five minutes, of which part is paid at the normal rate and the other part is simply not paid at all. This regime was imposed from the beginning of September to the middle of November, then suspended by the management (was there a reduction in orders?). The daily shift was changed back to nine and a quarter hours. It was thought that the so-called debt from May 1968 (as though the workers could have "debts" vis-à-vis the management!) was paid off.

Illusion.

At the break a crowd formed in front of the small printed text of the notice. Murmurings. Some men have it translated for them. Astonishment, confusion. "Again!" say expressions and gestures.

"As of Monday, February 17, 1969, the work shift will be increased to ten hours, the end of the shift being extended to 17:45 hours. The start remains fixed at 07 hours and the dinner break at 45 minutes. Half of the 45 minutes of extra work will be unpaid, in order to provide reimbursement of the advances allowed to the work force during May and June 1968."

We read it again and again, as though there were a secret clause. Yet it's not difficult to understand. They've decided that we will work ten hours a day again, because that suits them, and of that time we will supply twenty minutes of work officially free of charge: and they're taking that in addition to everything else!

And if you don't like it: get out.

Primo, cut to the quick, at once dashed off to see the delegate in whom he had the most confidence, Klatzman, to ask him how the CGT intended to react. Klatzman is a worker-priest, discreet and devoted, but overwhelmed. He thinks of his task as a series of interventions to be carried out one at a time in an attempt to settle the most scandalous cases rather than to lead an agitation. His slow manner of speech, his hesitation over the choice of words, make him seem timid, which he isn't. In confronting the factory management he's not lacking in firmness. Klatzman is honest, I'm sure, but I find him too inclined to respect the union hierarchy to take any vigourous initiative. I prefer other worker-priests in the thirteenth arrondissement, grassroots militants in their factories, ardent admirers of Che Guevara, desperate for justice and action, and I sometimes go to see them in search of courage and advice.

Klatzman promised Primo to bring up the question of recuperation at the next office meeting of the CGT. The reply came two days later. Klatzman, who was somewhat embarrassed, had to explain to Primo that after consultation with the CGT branches in the other Citroën factories (the "recuperation" was due to affect them also from February 17th onward) it had appeared that they were not strong enough to allow action. The unions had already called for a rejection of the recuperation in the autumn of 1968, and it had ended in failure: a few militants had stopped work, but there was no follow-up. There could be no repetition of such operations, which would discourage the grassroots union members. What was more, the situation was difficult for the action committee: the CFT, supported by the blackmail and pressure systems available to the management, was becoming more and more of a threat, and the slightest tactical error by the CGT could risk compromising the future elections at the CE. In short, the union would do nothing. Primo retorted that the call in the autumn of 1968 had lacked conviction, to say the least, and that on each "national day of action by metal-workers", the union had in fact called out workers knowing very well that their stoppage would not be carried out by more than thirty men. That this time there was something much more serious at stake, and that if the management were allowed to do what they liked without any reaction, this would encourage the CFT, etc. Klatzman indicated to him with a helpless gesture that the decision did not come from him and, whatever his personal opinion, he couldn't change anything.

The canteen. Primo describes this interview to me. He doesn't usually lose his self-control but this time his lively gestures shake the table. "Look, it's not possible! We can't just take it!" Yes, definitely, something must be done. We're pressed for time. Workers with trays are waiting to sit down. We give up our places. See you tonight, on the way out.

All afternoon I chew over plans, inattentive to my mechanical movements. "Something wrong?" asks Simon between two trips, surprised to see me so preoccupied. I tell him that I'm furious at soon having to work ten hours a day again. So's he. And, he adds, everyone is fed up; he's already heard several conversations about it.

I meet Primo again in the pub. We go into a corner in order to talk in peace.

Out of this discussion comes the plan to organize ourselves independently of the union, to get together all those opposed to the recuperation and go on strike when the day comes. With the help of comrades outside, including Yves, whom Primo already knows, I will run off and distribute leaflets which we will draw up ourselves.

I explain to Primo my personal situation, the fact that I've "established" myself in this job to contribute to the workers' struggle within the factory. He's not surprised. He's already heard talk about this "establishment" system, and he thinks it's a good thing. It can help to widen the workers' horizons and bring the intellectuals in the revolutionary groups—who are too inclined to abstractions—down to earth. Each side will gain from it. And the sympathy of young people for the working class doesn't leave him unmoved: students have changed, there are now some heirs to the bourgeoisie who reject their privileges and choose the other camp. Primo sees these new things with hope. But what counts, obviously, is what people will succeed in doing as concrete acts.

We make a rapid list of everyone whom we can contact. Primo thinks he can count on five or six colleagues from the paint shop, and on a few others scattered around the works. On my side, I'll speak to Christian, Simon, the Yugoslavs, and my friends from Gravier's shop. We have only to fix a date for a meeting. We choose a Friday, for work finishes earlier that day and with the relief of the weekend it will be easier to obtain the necessary time from each man. We will meet at the Café des Sports, a big modern café gleaming with neon lights on the far side of the outer boulevards, where the owner happily lends his basement room to groups who want to meet, providing they buy drinks.

Now to arrange the meeting. I get on with it at once, taking advantage of the breaks, the canteen, and the cloakrooms, quickly making dates in the crush as the men pour in and out around the time clock. Often in the café.

At the same time I undertake to explain my "establishment" to all those I think I know sufficiently well. If we are to act together, it would be dishonest to conceal my situation.

I'd already talked about the "establishment" question to

Sadok, almost by accident, because it came up in conversation at the works. I'd told him that I wasn't really a worker and had completed my studies, which allowed me to be a teacher. He'd listened to me with an indulgent scepticism, visibly doubting that anyone could choose such a life without being forced to. Rather like the reaction of a prisoner to whom someone who's just arrived in the cell proclaims: "Mine's a special case, I'm innocent!" Go on, man, thinks the old inhabitant, we know that story. Then, when Sadok came to stay with me for a few days, after his landlord had thrown him out, he was convinced, once he saw the piles of books and papers.

"So you could really be a teacher or work in an office?"

"Yes."

He hadn't replied, but his eyes said: "You're out of your mind."

This extreme reaction from Sadok remained isolated. Most of the others were hardly affected by the situation. The Yugoslavs took it in without making the slightest comment. Simon said: "Oh, good. Are there many of you like that?" His mobile face assumed a hopeful expression, as though he were about to hear some good news. But I'd hardly answered before he began to talk about something else. As for Christian, he asked me questions about the situation in the colleges and the relationships between the revolutionary groups. And then, very quickly, my news passed into the general picture of individual characteristics to which, as a rule, no one pays attention any more. Nobody spoke to me about it again.

In the outside world the "establishment" appears spectacular, the papers make it into quite a legend. Seen from the works, it's not very important in the long run. Everyone who works here has a complex individual story, often more fascinating and more embroiled than that of the student who has temporarily turned worker. The middle classes always imagine they have a monopoly on personal histories. How ridiculous! They have a monopoly on speaking in public, that's all. They spread themselves. The others live their stories with intensity, but in silence. Nobody is born a semiskilled worker, you become one. And here, in the works, it's very rare to refer to someone as "the worker who ..." No. They say: "The person who works in the soldering shop," "The person who works on the fenders." The person. I'm neither the "worker" nor the man who's "established" himself. I'm "the person who works on the gantry crane". And my particular distinction of being "established" takes its place in a harmless way in the tangle of destinies and special cases.

The only real difference between me and my workmates—they include a good number of improvised workers who've come from the country or from overseas—is that I can always revert to my status as an intellectual. I live through my suffering like them, but I remain free to fix its duration. I'm very much aware of this difference, as of a particular responsibility. I can't remove it. However severe the repression, it will never affect me as much as it does them.

I promise myself to stay in the factory as long as I can without being fired, whatever the result of our struggle, however bad the repression. Whatever happens, I won't hand in my notice.

Friday, half-past four. There are about twenty of us at the meeting in the basement of the Café des Sports.

As he promised, Primo has brought a few workmates from the paint shop. I'll be seeing one of them frequently later on: Mohamed. When he was a shepherd in Kabylia he fell in love with poetry and began to study and to teach himself. He came to Paris in the hope of studying literature. No family, no fellowship, no support of any kind, he didn't have a chance. He became a semiskilled worker with Citroën. His gentle and strangely studied manner of speech recalls his literary plans. He's very young; he seems shy. Primo introduced him to me as one of the most militant men in the paint shop.

Georges and five other Yugoslavs are there. Simon, too.

Sadok arrived late. I think he wanted to be certain there were other people at the meeting before taking part in it himself. He looked furtively down from the stairs, gave me a smile which expressed greeting and apologies, and came down, sitting at the back.

Mouloud isn't here. When I went to tell him about it he had said he wouldn't come but that he agreed with us, and that if there was a strike against the recuperation, he'd join it.

Several of the workers present are unknown to me: Spaniards, Blacks from Mali and Senegal.

Christian's come with a French friend, Jean-Louis, a young, fair-haired southerner who wears a little beard. They're very close and very unlike. While Christian, who's a bundle of nerves, is always on the brink of violent confrontation with the Citroën system, Jean-Louis pursues his life with care. One foot in the CGT union, which hopes to put him up for the elections of staff delegates; one foot in the Citroën channel for internal promotion, where he attends a course in the evenings in the hope of becoming a craftsman. He lives in a tough Citroën hostel, where the warden is a former army man. He tries to work his way around all obstacles and avoids attracting attention to himself. He's come more from friendship for Christian and curiosity than in opposition to the "recuperation". He hardly speaks during the meeting, except to say that it would be a good thing to let the CGT branch know about our action. With which everyone agrees.

The meeting is short.

Primo and I explain the point of it: to organize rejection of the recuperation through a strike, and to prepare for a stoppage every day at five o'clock in the afternoon from February 17th on.

The first thing to do is to contact as many people as possible. Therefore we must draw up a leaflet. What does everyone think?

Georges speaks first. He says he's in agreement, but he's sceptical about the result. Without wasting time on general considerations he describes the situation as we can reasonably foresee it. He thinks that he himself can bring together a fairly large number of Yugoslavs. In any case Stepan, Pavel, and he will stop at five o'clock on February 17th, and they're certain they can carry two Portuguese from the "roundabout" with them: in that way they will stop the production of doors. Good. But there are reserve stocks for much more than three-quarters of an hour. So that won't stop shop number 85. Simon and I will stop the gantry crane. But any boss or adjustor will replace us at once, and will immediately re-establish the distribution of component parts on the main assembly line. The upholstery shop won't cause any stoppage either. Naturally Christian will stop making his seats, but that won't have any immediate effect in view of the reserve stock, even if the Algerian and the Black working beside him stop, too (it seems very unlikely that the woman will stop). Conclusion: this is not enough. The essential thing, in shop 85, is the big assembly line. If that stops, we've won. If not, all the other stoppages will not hold up production. Now, at this meeting, who is there from the big assembly line? No one. Between now and the next meeting we must aim above all to contact people from the big line, without whom our attempts will remain in the air. In the meantime, Georges is curious to know precisely on whom we can count in the other shops. Not only in global figures but from the point of view of holding up production. Because if everywhere else is like shop 85 ...

At which he stubs out his English cigarette and says no more.

Silence.

His little speech has been like a cold shower.

Twenty people out of twelve hundred—let's say forty, counting those we're already sure of having with us—obviously it's not many. Vaguely we knew this, and Georges has just made us consciously aware of the physical situation. The works is a monster to be stopped. And what if it went quietly on its way, unmoved by our agitation?

Georges is right. A real strike means blocking production and making them lose 2 CVs. If we succeed in doing this we'll really strike a blow at the management, one that will mean something to everyone. If not, we'll be crushed, people will lose heart, the Citroën system will be reinforced as a result.

A round of the shops. It's soon done. Nobody from the presses. Primo thinks they can stop the paint shop completely, provided they can come to an agreement with the few militant craftsmen who belong to the CGT. What about Gravier's soldering shop? Sadok pulls a face. A Tunisian with a pockmarked face, a solderer in number 86, also appears doubtful. Gravier is feared; the shop is small and under constant supervision. The drivers? Nobody. The hoist men? The "takers-away", who remove and park the finished cars? Nobody. These are key posts, through which we can hope to stop internal movement. We've got no hold for the moment.

In fact, all the work still has to be done.

This strike has to be built up. Patiently. Job by job. Man by man. Shop by shop. It's the first time I see the question from this angle. The class war at trench level. Lampman's level.

Then Christian intervenes. Suppose a determined group were to go and cut off the electricity at the start of the main assembly line at five o'clock precisely, and be ready, too, to defend themselves against the bosses who would try to switch it on again?

Georges condemns the proposition with a single gesture. And then what? That will mean six or seven people fired on the spot for causing a scuffle inside the works, and we couldn't even be certain of stopping production for more than five minutes. In any case, if the people want to recuperate, you can't stop them from doing it. That's their concern. No, we have to come to an agreement with enough people to stop the factory, that's all.

There's no answer. We have to get on with it.

Primo: "Well, we've got one month. On the big line in

number 85 there are Algerians, Moroccans, Tunisians, Yugoslavs, Spaniards, Portuguese, Malians, workmates from other countries as well. Let's get together a good leaflet to explain to them what we want to do. And let's make translations into all the languages on the line, so that everyone who can read understands and can tell the others what's being said. After that we'll go and see them one at a time to discuss it."

This idea of leaflets in several languages appeals to everyone. It has more than a utilitarian function. It's a mark of respect toward all the cultures represented in the factory. It's a way of asking the different immigrant communities to take things in hand.

Now we must draw up the text. Why we reject the recuperation. Explanations come from all sides. We can talk about the fatigue caused by the ten-hour days. Those who have an hour's journey to work and back no longer have any life outside the factory. Fatigue increases accidents. Every change of time schedule is a reason for intensifying the speed of work. Why not take advantage of it to mention particular claims again? Qualification for the paint workers and solderers. Mention also the unhealthy areas. And what about the racism among the bosses? And payment for overtime? Hey, it's not a leaflet we're going to draw up any more, it's a book ...

Primo again: "Look, it's not worth telling all those stories. If the boss wants to make us work for ten hours again with twenty minutes unpaid, it's in order to humiliate us. They want to show us that the big strikes are all over, and that Citroën's doing what they want. It's an attack on our dignity. What are we? Dogs? 'Do this, do that, and shut up!' It doesn't work! We're going to show them that they can't treat us like that. It's a question of honor. Everyone can understand that, can't they? That's the only thing to say, that's enough!"

The contents of the leaflet have been found. On the edge of the table I write out briefly what Primo has just said in one spurt. We read it. Two or three words are changed, final version: everyone approves. The leaflet will be translated into Arabic, Spanish, Portuguese, Yugoslav. Fleetingly it occurs to me that these words ring out strongly in all languages: "insult", "pride", "honor" ...

We will run off a thousand copies of the French version in order to distribute it at the main entrance. We will run off a hundred copies of the translations into each language: we will display these leaflets everywhere in the works, in the cloakrooms and workshops, and we will circulate them from hand to hand.

There has to be a signature. We decide to put: "The Shop Floor Committee, Citroën-Choisy."

We'll meet again next Friday, more of us if possible, in order to see where we are.

It's over. We go up again. The Café des Sports hums with the noise of a Friday evening. Smoke. Loud voices, shouts, and laughter. Groups of people gather busily, preparing the racing bets. Greetings are exchanged.

The street. It's very cold. The snow falls damply on the slippery pavement. Night has already come down over the boulevards, where a weekend stream of cars is dashing along. On the other side, the factory is no more than a dark mass. Inert until Monday. The workmates hurry toward the metro, turning up the collars of their coats and jackets.

I remain motionless for a moment, suddenly drained. By the week, by the meeting. I think: that's it. Is it going to last? An early throbbing tremor. The fight which is starting here, now. This collectivity that's forming. So many hopes ... It's intoxicating.

"And now, we're going to have that spaghetti, are we?"

Primo takes me by the elbow, smiling. It's true, we had decided to have dinner together at my place this evening.

Let's go.

We construct our strike.

I discover that the gantry crane is a strategic position. The parts of the coachwork that Simon will share out along the big assembly line start from here. From now on the leaflets will follow the same route. Simon, who's delighted, stuffs them under his jacket with the gestures of a conspirator. This underground work suits him perfectly. He's taken the hoods, he brings his cart back empty: the Spaniards have got their leaflets. A trip with doors: the leaflets in Arabic have gone to the Moroccan working on the front lights. He whispers the details to me, describes the reactions in detail. At snack time we stand aside to take stock.

The leaflets have made a deep impression. It's our dignity they want to destroy by this unpaid extra work, they repeat every day in all languages; it's more important than fatigue, pay, and everything else; it's beyond price!

The Black working on the seats has read it in Arabic, slowly, then he comes to shake my hand. He'll stop at five o'clock, he promises.

We put up the leaflet everywhere. The john's an excellent place: people can read in peace, sheltered from onlookers.

It's beginning to bite a little along the big assembly line. Here or there is a promise to stop at five o'clock. Will that be enough?

At the second meeting of the shop floor committee there are about thirty of us. We take stock, we count, we face the reactions, we go through the reasons put forward by those who are hesitant, we prepare answers. We draw up a list of posts which are hard to hold and are important in production, those which Citroën will find difficult to get going again in two minutes if there should be a stoppage.

My memories of this period are of natural, almost peaceable, functioning. And I think that most of the workmates felt the same. The ordinary occupations of the struggle freed us partly from anxiety and bitterness. Everything was taking on a meaning. For once the hurts and humiliations of daily life were not lost in the bottomless well of our impotent rage. The bosses could insult, push, steal, lie. We had opened a secret attack on them and each time that they made it worse with a new injustice, we thought: rendezvous on February 17th.

At last we had a common horizon; we acquired the habit of enlarging it. In the morning, during the 8:15 break, we would install ourselves on the third step of the iron staircase which goes up from our shop to the paint shop. There, among the grease stains and the unwrapped sandwiches, we would hold little political meetings, six or seven of us. I remember clearly one of these conversations, and a remark by Georges. Simon was getting excited thinking about the coming revolution: "We'll have to attack the barracks straightaway, to get weapons ..." Georges interrupted him, sneering slightly: "In cases like this it's not weapons that are lacking, but the courage to use them. You can always find weapons ..." Simon gave a curious imitation of a schoolboy who's made a mistake, and was silent.

With the distribution of the leaflets, our little gatherings in the shop, the meetings of the shop floor committee, the feverish checking of our progress, this month of propaganda was on the whole a month of happiness.

4

The strike

Monday, February 17th, five minutes to five.

Is it going to be O.K.? I'm sweating, and it's not fatigue from work. Breathing difficult, dull pounding in my chest: anxiety.

At this precise moment the idea of defeat is unbearable to me. Reasons jostle each other in my head. The half-deaf men at the presses, the gas-poison cases in the paint shop, the CFT informers, the searches by the guards, Junot's blackmailing, the minutes stolen from the breaks, the bribery of industrial medicine ... To attack them in their puffed-up confidence and insolence, the Graviers, Junots, Duprés, Huguets, Bineaus, and all those from up above whom we don't even see!

Two minutes to five.

For the sake of honor, Primo said. For the sake of dignity, we've put in the leaflets. In the long run all strikes come back to this. To show that they haven't succeeded in breaking us. That we remain free men.

It has to work, the factory must stop. I study faces. How can one know? Have we explained sufficiently what's at stake? Perhaps we should have done hand-outs at the doors of the hostels. Or a special meeting perhaps for the drivers? Yes, but through whom to contact them? Big Marcel? Not very talkative. Are the Malians going to stop, as they have apparently said?

Provided the bosses don't start intimidation immediately! I look around me. No blue coat. No white coat. They're getting at us through scorn: we don't give a damn about your leaflets; the factory won't stop, because we've got it well under control; if twenty or thirty of you put down your tools we'll replace you and the 2 CVs will go out normally. Yes, scorn. But I'm sure they're on watch in their glass-walled cages, ready to rush along if there's trouble.

Georges makes a sign to me. Only thirty seconds. The din of the shop is at full blast. Stridence, shouts, gimlets, screws, braces, hammers, files, sanding machines, drills, fork lifts ...

Only a few more seconds.

That's it. Five o'clock.

I stop the crane and take off my gloves. Slowly, obviously, to make it clear around me that I'm stopping work. Simon's standing still too. The noise? It seems to be lessening. A glance at the door roundabout: it's stopped. Georges is putting down his tools. Stepan and Pavel are packing up. I listen as hard as I can to the main assembly line. Yes, it's making less and less noise. From post to post I see men leaving it.

Still a few sounds of gimlets and hammering, isolated.

And silence.

Oh, this silence, how it echoes in our heads!

It's one minute past five. The main assembly line workshop has stopped.

But that's not all. We have to be quick. A few dozen workers have left their positions. The gaps have stopped the line. But many others have stayed in place, uncertain. They're not working any more, but they're waiting. Already bosses, adjustors, and foremen appear from every-where and get busy. Adjustors and charge hands are going to replace the missing men and try to start up the machines again. Now we must give the stoppage a bigger twist, before they succeed. Georges and the Yugoslavs have understood. Christian too, who's making tracks as fast as he can. And here we are in a little procession of about fifty workers, descending on the main assembly line, going from post to post, to convince our mates to stop work once and for all and go to the cloakrooms.

"Come on, stop, come with us. You can see there's a blockage everywhere. And then, from now on, you're working for the boss without pay. Don't let down your mates who've stopped!"

The assembly lines are beginning to look very empty. Some men go to the cloakrooms, others come to swell our procession. There's a buzz of talk. Everything's been stopped for three minutes now and they still haven't succeeded in starting up again.

"We must go to the transfer spot and try to make Theodoros stop," Georges says.

It's a key post, a difficult one: where the engine is fixed onto the chassis. The worker who does the job, Theodoros, is a Yugoslav. If he stops, the two sections making up the big assembly line are blocked. We run there. Here we are around him. Everyone talks at once. Georges begins again in Yugoslav, calmly, tries to convince him. He's afraid. That's what he replies to us, and it's obvious. He still has his tools in his hands, the long cable with the switch that maneuvers the transfer machine, the wrenches for the fixing. He remains as though petrified, speaking with difficulty. His eyes move from one point to another in the workshop. We've only been there a few seconds when the bosses appear. They've rushed along after us trying to make up for the effect of the demonstration and check the stoppage. Now they're pushing their way toward Theodoros. There's Huguet, knitting his brows and drawing himself up to his full height, which is short, Dupré, muttering something indistinctly, of which we can only make out "... this circus", and above all Junot, the section manager, red-faced, swollen with anger, almost apoplectic, barking: "Let people work! You're hindering the freedom to work! I'm taking names! I'm taking names! You haven't any right!" He's now very close to Theodoros. He tries to push us back, to get Georges out of the way. We're determined not to fight. We know very well that he wants it: one blow, one angry fist, and that will be it. But we stay there, massed together while he storms and raves, with his "freedom to work" on his lips.

At the moment I'm writing I retain this image: a pig wearing a tie, who's come from his armchair to yell about the right of "freedom to work" to a tired, anxious worker, whom Citroën has decided to rivet to the assembly line for three-quarters of an hour extra.

The worker hesitates, looks at the section manager, looks at us. He seems overwhelmed by events. Something akin to despair comes into his eyes for a moment. And then, all at once, Theodoros lets go of his tools and begins to yell: "Leave me alone! Leave me alone!" A kind of hysteria. He's very tall, agitated, and trembling. Junot's frightened and jumps back. A small blow in order to have a reason for firing him would be all right, but Junot has no wish at all to be beaten up!

Theodoros' wild cry has finally disorganized the assembly line. Workers come rushing up from all sides. Our little troop is suddenly swollen, the stoppage in the workshop is complete. Now thirty or so of our mates from the paint shop arrive down stairs. It's a real demonstration by some two hundred workers running through the idle factory. The machines are silent: our shouts are the only sounds to be heard.

We come out in a rush. Yves and friends from the outside are waiting impatiently. Excitement. It's worked. The whole factory's stopped. Meet later over the leaflets.

Hectic meeting at the Café des Sports. We check and re-check in the uproar of the basement. 84. 85. 86. All the workshops have come out. There are more than four hundred strikers. Not a single car came off the line after five o'clock. Now we've got to hold on. We draw up a leaflet: the number of strikers, an appeal. Translations again. The duplicator. Late at night everything's ready.

I can't sleep.
    Short catnaps torn apart by visions.
    The shantytowns march toward Neuilly.
    Great proletarian joy in the Champs-Elysées.

Our submerged world springs out and pours over the other one. Like a lost continent suddenly brought to light, and the tidal wave produced by its emergence. The old society, suffering lockjaw, incredulously watches the spread of an unknown, incomprehensible joy.

We will break open the walls of the factory to bring light and the outside world into it.

We'll organize our work, we'll produce other objects, we shall all be scholars and soldiers, writers and laborers. We shall invent new languages. We shall do away with degradation and routine. Sadok and Simon won't be afraid any longer. A dawn never seen before.

Wan and cold, the February dawn, the real one, cuts through the dream. I must go back. One single thought in my dulled movements: this evening, five o'clock.

Tuesday, February 18th.

The factory is planned to produce objects and crush men. This Tuesday morning, right from the start, the Citroën antistrike machine has been set in motion. Yesterday the bosses treated us with contempt. Today, a change of tactics: it's their presence. And what presence! The entire factory echoes with their shouts, their coming and going, their meddlesome interference. They come out of the walls. There were so many of them, then, lying low in their glass-walled lairs! Blue coats, white coats, grey coats, even the three-piece suits, arriving on various pretexts. Everything gives them an opportunity for nagging the workers: this soldering's no good! this spraying's good! this join's no good! this retouching's no good!

Nothing's any good any more.

We know what isn't any good: the strike yesterday. But for the moment they're not talking about it. They're harassing us as we work, and they stay there to intimidate us. They're highly visible, they watch us. We'll see whether, this evening at five o'clock, the mass of workers will dare to down tools again under their noses, a few feet away!

Junot looks in all directions and without any purpose, his

face has the congested expression of an alcoholic adjutant. He goes to speak to the guards, comes to study papers in the foreman's office, sets off again toward the time clock, comes back with a bundle of individual punched cards, and those who see him pass, his eyes plunged like this into the list of our names, can't stop themselves from wondering: what's he cooking up? Is it my card, my name, that he's looking at just now?

But he's merely doing his work! Isn't Junot the official head of the factory repression department? It's his job to break the strike: he's doing it. He's on the attack, at the head of his troops. On the alert, foremen and charge hands! On the alert, guards! On the alert, CFT, the yellow union! Citroën is mobilizing.

Noon. In the canteen we rapidly exchange news. Everywhere the same clearing of decks for action. Primo thinks the paint sprayers will keep up. The workmates from number 86 are less optimistic. Gravier, the foreman, and Antoine, the charge hand, are wild with fury. They're reacting like petty kings. They were surprised and angry at yesterday's stoppage, and they're determined to prevent it happening again this evening. They're pushing speed to the maximum, all over the place they're inventing badly done soldering jobs and insisting they be done again. They've even threatened a Tunisian with the sack for insufficient production. Similar details flood in from the other workshops. They're doing everything they can to make life wretched for us. Did the drivers stop yesterday? Well, they'll see. They continually find batteries for them to take out, containers to move, components to deliver. Transport jobs, which have been forgotten for a fortnight, become urgent. To be done in the next hour. The round trips made by the fork lifts have been frantic all morning. This unbridled traffic exasperates the drivers and threatens us at every move: you can't walk twenty yards in the shop without nearly causing an accident. And this afternoon it's obviously going to get worse, the drivers are so overwhelmed with the number of accumulated orders. All the laborers have had complaints at their own level. Even the sweepers are being worked to death: the foremen have promised each other to complain in chorus about some bit of rubbish they pretend they've discovered.

Our work, fragmented and split up into insignificant, infinitely repeated movements, can be torture. Sometimes we forget it, when the relative torpor and regularity of the workshop offer us the fragile resource of habit. But the bosses do *not* forget it. They know that the slightest increase of pressure, the slightest acceleration of speed, the slightest harassment on their part, shatters this thin shell where we sometimes take refuge. No more protection for anyone. And here we are with raw nerves, our fatigue increased by irritation, doing this semiskilled work under direct fire for what it is: unbearable.

All this agitation by the bosses is implied blackmail. Oh, you're refusing to work three-quarters of an hour more? Very well. We're going to show you what we can do with the nine and a quarter hours when you're in our power: they'll count double, they'll wear you out much more than the ten "normal" hours we'd like to impose on you! We'll see all right who'll be worn out first. (A few months later, the foreman Gravier will speak to me openly like this: "You're patient, but we're more patient than you are: we'll see who'll be worn out first." Meaning: we have endless ways of making life impossible for you and forcing you to leave.)

The system functions in accordance with strict logic: work is exhausting, but a strike is even more so. The physical fatigue of the ten hours? Perhaps. But no complications. Open the path to submission as the easy way out. Wherever do they find these techniques of power, which are so precise?

We've spent the morning trying to contain this compression. Distributing the leaflets, discussing. Taking advantage of the breaks. Trying to revive the thrill of yesterday evening: "We really got them, didn't we? Did you see their faces? And it'll be the same tonight!"

Every two hours the paint sprayers have a ten-minute break, in a so-called rest room (a few iron chairs in a dirty recess, a slight distance away from the chemical vapors): along with a glass of milk per day, as a pretense at checking the physiological deterioration which everyone knows to be inevitable. Primo has turned these breaks to advantage by dashing from one point to another in the factory, to every place where he knows people.

But we have to be careful. Supervision is strict.

Georges has made use of the break to go to Gravier's shop to talk to two Spanish solderers. He hadn't been there a minute before Gravier leaped out of his office like a jack-in-the-box, and ordered him to beat it ("What's all this about! This isn't a gossip shop, I don't want any outsider here in the workshop!"). Georges left casually, an ironic smile on his lips, but without knowing what the two Spaniards will do this evening. He was struck by the tense atmosphere which hovered over shop 86. Nobody was saying a word. A solid silence.

Fortunately Simon, through the coming and going of his carts of components, has kept contact with the main assembly line. We've checked the numbers again: there are some defections, but on the whole it looks as though it's holding. Some nonstrikers from yesterday have even announced that they would join us this evening.

Tuesday afternoon. As soon as work began again there were newcomers on the scene: the interpreters.

Ah, you can fatten people up, with the surplus from the assembly line workers!

The Citroën interpreters ... Smartly dressed, relaxed, possessing the gift of gab, these middle-class Moroccans, Yugoslavs, and Spaniards are the agents of a formidable system. Residence permits, work permits, contracts, social security, allowances, everything goes through them. For the immigrants who don't speak French, or speak it badly, the house interpreters constitute an obligatory passage to official society, which is so complicated, so confusing, with its formulae, its offices and mysterious rules. The interpreter gentleman will sort that out for you. The interpreter gentleman is your friend, the spokesman in your language of the boss's benevolence.

Today this "assistant" reveals his true colors.

They have spread through all the shops. Going from post to post they enter into conversation with the strikers. The same little speech in every language: "Listen, Mohamed (or Miklos, or M'Ba, or Gonçalves, or Manuel), yesterday you did something silly: you know very well that work stops at a quarter to six and that you haven't got the right to leave at five. O.K., this time we'll take no notice. But if you do it again you're in for big trouble. And in the first place there'll be no point in coming to see me any more about a document, or to sort something out for you. If you walk out at five o'clock this evening I don't know you any more. Think it over carefully."

Terrible threat. Who can remain indifferent to it?

No interpreter any more: you find yourself suddenly in the dark, deaf and dumb, incapable of the slightest move, rejected by the administration, by the whole of society. How can you escape in the future the thousand and one pitfalls of French bureaucracy, the crushing inertia of a hostile world?

"If you walk out at five o'clock, I don't know you any more."

They've got a list. They go methodically from striker to striker. They're in a good mood, at their ease. They speak several languages, no doubt they're studying law or have a university education behind them. They're training to be civil servants or police officers in their own country, if they aren't to that stage already. These middle-class types come as far as this to break the strikes by proletarians from their own country. As I see them operating with such gentle insinuation I feel a kind of nausea.

There's one twenty yards away from me, very near the crane. He's in the process of "doing" the door roundabout. He's sunburnt, with black hair, and he's starting to put on weight, he's assumed the expression of a second-rate film actor—a fixed smile, showing his white teeth. His brown suit is slightly open over a little waistcoat, he puts across his story with the gestures of an insurance salesman and ends with a paternal pat on the shoulder for the worker, who works in silence.

Abject.

That's how the antistrike machine works. It started without any problem, as though switched on automatically by the warning on Monday evening. It was there, oiled, ready for service, lurking beneath the row made by the others, beneath the corresponding structures of iron and steel. Oh, it's not working flat out yet! It has plenty of other resources, other mechanisms which the relay system has not yet put into operation: the rounding up of men, the firings, the entry of the police, the expulsion of the immigrant "agitators" to their own countries (and the fellow whom the inspectors come to take away from the section manager's office will find himself twenty-four hours later in the prisons of Franco or Hassan II), the witch-hunt in the hostels ... Everyone knows that the mechanism exists, that it's happened before and will happen again. It's simply held in reserve. For the moment it's purring gently, the antistrike machine with harassment at work, the mobilization of the bosses, blackmail by the interpreters, the threats. The routine.

That's how cars are produced. Machines mold the sheet iron, others knead the human material. The factory is a whole. The men and women in the shop work in silence, and their faces say nothing. It's on them that the net of circumstances weighs now. How can this resistance be measured? We'll know at five o'clock.

As the time approaches tension increases. I can see it in people's looks. We exchange questions in silence. What will my neighbor do? What will I do? Collect one's willpower, take one's decision. We keep our eyes open for the charge hand, the foreman, well in sight, a few yards away, so near ...

And then it goes very quickly. Five o'clock, departures from all sides to the cloakrooms, immobilization of the assembly lines. In a few seconds a third of the shop has emptied. Those who remain cannot start again: too many gaps to fill. Shouts break out. The foreman Huguet has posted himself at the exit and calls to a group of Blacks who are leaving: "Listen, it's not time yet! You'll hear from me!" Dupré on his side is making a fuss in upholstery. Too late. The wave of strikers flows out in silence.

I feel a sudden rush of admiration in my chest.

Once again the Café des Sports and its smoke-filled basement. We immediately regain our lair, we crowd into it. Take stock. We've all felt the difference in this silent stoppage. Yesterday there was an explosion of delight, chaos, surprise at being so many. Today each striker left his post without a word, without a gesture. Faces were grave. All day we felt we were being spied upon. Discussions were relegated to the johns, or the corners of corridors. The works has drawn back: only whisperings on our side, while the voice of the management has not stopped ringing out and occupying the terrain. It's like a vice which has been in place since the morning: today, Tuesday, first turn of the screw. What will the second one be?

Shop by shop we count up the strikers. More than three hundred. A hundred fewer than yesterday, it's not many in the end, after all this mobilization of the bosses. But after all it's a setback. The movement isn't developing. We were dreaming of a snowball effect. But we're forced to see that we reached the maximum the first day: now an erosion is setting in. Another blow: apart from Choisy, nothing's happened in the Citroën factories in the Paris area. Recuperation has begun everywhere else, without a hitch. We're isolated.

How can we regain the lost territory? The comrades give their opinions one after the other. Primo the Sicilian, Georges the Yugoslav, Sadok the Algerian, Christian the Breton, Boubakar the Malian... It's the Kabylian shepherd from the paint shop, Mohamed, who speaks longest, in his even voice, with his strange way of choosing literary words. Tomorrow morning we'll talk to the Monday strikers who didn't down tools today; perhaps we'll be able to swim against the tide, counteract to some extent the effect of the threats from the management. But that isn't enough. We must try to broaden the base of the movement, seek out all possible support. Last week the CGT branch distributed a leaflet attacking the recuperation. They didn't demonstrate on Monday and Tuesday. He, Mohamed, is prepared to go and see them on behalf of the shop floor committee and ask them to speak in the canteen at noon. The staff delegates can represent legal protection, a means of help.

We agree to ask the delegates to speak.

Another thing. We'll try to have discussions with the adjustors and some charge hands. The Yugoslavs suggest drawing up a leaflet for the technical managers. We would appeal to them not to play strikebreakers. Animated discussion. Some think it's useless. Christian says that the majority of the bosses belong to the CFT: they're official strikebreakers. Yes, but not all. It's important to show that we know how to tell the difference and recognize the bosses who remain relatively neutral. In the end the idea of the leaflet is adopted on the basis of a compromise proposed by Primo: we will denounce by name the bosses who have gone in for open intimidation and who hurled threats at workers who were walking out at five o'clock. But at the same time we'll speak to the whole of the senior staff, the management representatives, the charge hands, the adjustors, and we'll say to them: your work should not be work of intimidation; it's a question of dignity for you as well. The right to strike exists. Going on strike is a matter of conscience which affects everyone. Respect the workers who walk out at five o'clock.

Difficult to write it.

The meeting's been long, with much detail and repetition. Fatigue undermines us, expanding people's remarks. They can't hear properly, they're getting irritable,

they talk loudly ... O.K. It's over, it remains to put things
into practice. Mohamed and Simon will set off in search of
Klatzman during the night (he lives in an HLM at Ivry).
Primo, Christian, and I will duplicate leaflets with Yves.

Stencils. Typing errors. Retyping.

The duplicator. Its regular purring. I feel I'm hearing a
train running quietly through the darkness. Images of
elsewhere.

The night sways among smells of ink and the rustle of
sheets of paper.

And suddenly it's already morning.

Outside the works, a quarter to seven. The over-wakeful
quivering of mornings that follow sleepless nights. Acute,
anxious perception of sounds, faces, the lights from the
ending darkness. The metal of the main door, the slippery
ridge of the pavement, the symmetrical mass of the factory
buildings, the silent procession of men arriving, the thin
clouds of breath and cigarette smoke in the frozen air.

We hand out our leaflets.

It happens all at once. Like a blow in the stomach.

Four men rush up. Brutality. Leaflets flying. A fall on the
pavement. Blows. Parkas gleaming in the darkness. Shouts.
They yell: "Get the hell out of here! The workers want to
work!" I've recognized one face, an adjustor from the
pressing shop. We rush up. I get a glimpse of Christian
locked in a fight with one man, Yves with another. I seize
hold of a lapel, a thick face appears, twisted with hate, then
disappears at once into the crush. Movements. Workers
weigh in for us. I hear: "It's the bosses, oafs from the CFT!"
Also: "Someone's hurt!" One of the men distributing the
leaflets is bleeding. Another tears himself out of the struggle
and is protecting his bundle of leaflets. Someone shouts to
the men: "You aren't workers, you're spies for the
management!" They're beaten back, they go into the
factory, threatening: "There'll be more of us next time and
we'll get you!"

Panting after the fight.

We straighten our crumpled clothes.

The fellow who's bleeding has put a handkerchief over his forehead.

The distribution goes on.

Gradually breathing becomes calmer.

Second turn of the screw: the day will be tough.

Junot begins the attack again at half-past seven.

The place where I unload the gantry crane is situated at the entrance to the workshop, just opposite the section manager's office. From my post I can see, a few yards away, the reinforced green metal cage, topped with opaque panes of glass, which protrudes from the shop wall.

About half-past seven, then, there begins a little game that intrigues me. An adjustor replaces the Malian working on chassis on the main assembly line, and sends him to the office. The Malian passes slowly in front of me and hesitantly enters the glass cage. Two or three minutes later I see him come out again, looking totally crushed, and go back to his place. Next the adjustor relieves a Portuguese from the door roundabout. The office. The fellow looks horrible when he comes out. Then it's time for Stepan, the Yugoslav on the locks, whom I see coming back with set jaws, breathing rapidly from anger. Another. Yet another.

At the 8:15 break I rush to get news. The strikers are being called in one by one. The section manager has said the same thing to all of them: it's illegal to leave their post at five o'clock in the evening. "Do you know at least what 'contract of employment' means in French? You'd do well to find out. We're not a country of savages here, there are laws." Conclusion: in such cases the management has the right to fire people without warning. And as for the worker who lives in a Citroën hostel, he's reminded that this is a kindness on the part of the management, which is free to end it at once. "Be careful, France has welcomed you, but you must respect its laws. You may go."

Only the immigrants are called. In any case, they're the overwhelming majority.

All morning I see them follow each other, one by one, into Junot's office. Each time I imagine the scene taking place behind the opaque glass. The section manager seated comfortably in his armchair, behind his papers, his tweed jacket unbuttoned. The man stands awkwardly in front of him, in his dirty clothes, he still carries traces of the line he just left, he's caught in this unequal tête-à-tête.

What attitude should he take? Look the section manager in the eye? He'll take it as provocation. Hang his head, look at the floor? How can he accept this further humiliation? Let his eyes move to the left, to the right, look into the distance? Typical, isn't it, these immigrants who all have shifty eyes: you can't trust these people ... And coming from the section manager, the formal manner of address—he uses the proper *vous* with them—is in itself an implied threat. Unlike the bosses and the foremen who hail you in any old way (and without any politeness), Junot calls you by your surname and takes care to say *vous*. "Watch your step, Monsieur Benhamoud ..." Don't misunderstand. There's no hint of respect in this. Besides, everything else in his attitude and his remarks treats you, the whole time, as a "dirty wog". No, if he speaks to you in this unusually ceremonious fashion it's to make you recognize in his admonition the official language of registered letters with signatures for recorded delivery. Warnings, punishments, dismissal.

As the men come out I try to guess the result from each face. Will he stay with us? Or won't he? This one seems in a state of collapse. Another one shows by his face that it's anger which seems to predominate. Here's another who comes out with a shrug of his shoulders, he's a fatalist. Georges moves away with a sneer and takes time to stop and light a cigarette. One Algerian comes out so upset that he seems hesitant about which way to go in order to regain his post, and wanders aimlessly about the shop for a few moments.

By noon, thirty or so workers have been in. Others are waiting their turn. Vague anxiety.

Canteen. The approach to the CGT branch by Mohamed and Simon has been successful. A delegate will speak. Here he is, pushing his way through, a man of big build in a leather jacket. It's Boldo, a French craftsman, a big talker and an old hand at the works. He shouts a few words, so that everyone can hear him. He denounces the intimidation maneuvers, recalls that striking is legal and asks the workers to keep the delegates informed of violations of the right to strike in the different workshops. He's heard in a silence broken only by the sounds of trays and chairs as new men arrive. As soon as he's finished the hubbub breaks out again and at each table improvised translators explain what he's said. Every half hour he makes the same speech again, in order to keep up with the rapid rotation of the workers from different workshops in the cafeteria.

At last! the CGT has taken the plunge, for the first time since the start of the strike. We know that there was a lively discussion in the branch office. Some did not want to hear about this action, launched by the "extreme left". Galice, one of the responsible men in the branch, the most virulent as far as we are concerned, attacked "these students who come to give lessons to the working class" (he himself is a time-clerk foreman in the work-study office). But in the end a majority emerged to give support to the strike. The fellows from the paint shop and Klatzman carried the motion. Old Jojo, my neighbor in the cloakroom, even made a point of telling me that he supported us and had insisted that the union should be in evidence.

This intervention by the CGT will no doubt give a kind of legal backing to our strike in the eyes of a certain number of workers. It's important. But will it be enough to remove the threats which the management is making, with ever-increasing precision, to each striker? Doubtful.

In the afternoon Junot continues. Summons. Dressing down. "You may go."

His method is simple and effective. Every striker has to be individually sought out and got at. Remove him from the relative protection of collective action, during which he may believe he's lost in the crowd, almost anonymous. Let him hear his name called. Let him see it ringed in red on the list in Junot's possession. Let him feel, if only for a few seconds, the entire Citroën machine weighing down on him alone, within the four walls of this bare, metallic office, echoing with the roar of the nearby assembly lines.

Three hundred recalcitrants, it's still a lot. A quarter of the factory, more if one counts only the workers. So they're attacking the surface, point by point, in order to detach a few elements first. Reduce this mass. In two or three minutes each one of those who pass through Junot's office feels the plane going over him. There are so many words, in the language of production, to describe this levelling operation: planing, squaring off, trimming, sanding, filing, laminating ... Planks of wood, blocks of stone, slabs of steel, sheets of iron. And for man, this particular substance with which Junot is dealing, what word do you use?

Another section on the front: the bosses. Has our leaflet had any effect in that quarter? During the breaks in work we try to calculate its impact. In Simon's opinion some of the bosses have calmed down. Not the foremen, obviously. At this level, supreme in the workshop hierarchy, there are only committed supporters of the Citroën system. Huguet in 85, Gravier in 86, their opposite numbers in the paint shop and the pressing shop, pursue their policy of harassment without any weakening: being present, shouting, multiplying the number of rejected parts and extra bits of work. But lower down, at the level of charge hands and adjustors, there seems to be a certain ambivalence. Dupré has appeared a little more discreet than yesterday. And the red-haired, Irish-looking adjustor from 85 (the one who introduced me, without success, to the sheathing of windows) even whispered to Simon, while chewing an imaginary pipe and swallowing half his words: "... Don't give a damn, myself ... five o'clock, a quarter to six ... not my business ... I'm there for the work, myself, not for the time schedules ..." Simon reported these words to us triumphantly during the 3:15 break. Georges pointed out to him that this adjustor has always been eccentric. We mustn't have too many illusions. We'll have to see what the bosses will do at five o'clock. Vague hope, all the same, that they will be less threatening than yesterday at the time of the walk-out. All the more so since they all heard immediately that the union had spoken in the canteen against the acts of intimidation by the bosses.

As five o'clock approaches and the last moments of intense waiting begin, it's impossible to tell what will happen. Have we moved up the hill again? Or, on the contrary, have Junot and his men succeeded in intimidating a sufficient number of workers to make the strike collapse? And if there were a general upsurge, even more strikers than on the first day? Sometimes I find myself dreaming of this flow of men which would make Citroën give way and force them to give up the recuperation ... No. Reason. Assess. But this Wednesday, the center of gravity for the week, our strike has become complicated by so many interventions and incidents! The CFT attack on our hand-out of leaflets this morning, the planing-down operation by the section manager, the threat of expulsion from the hostels, of firing, the speech by the CGT in the canteen, the opposition moves within the union branch, the contradictory rumors about the state of mind among the bosses. And the nervous strain of these repeated stoppages, the effort of will in repeating them every evening, the fatigue which accumulates as the week goes on. I turn over and over in my mind the constituent factors in the situation. The result? It's present in each one of these heads bent over work on the line, all showing the exhaustion of the end of the day and anxiety about the decision to be taken.

Five o'clock.

The foremen stand near the doors again, threatening, reinforced by some charge hands. Calling out to those who are leaving.

The stoppage. Rapid, complete, silent. The shop's partly

empty. Enough to stop the lines. A little less massive than yesterday, I think.

The Café des Sports, the figures. About two hundred and fifty strikers. They have planed away fifty workmates from us.

More leaflets. The week's almost over, hold on, go around the situation shop by shop; we insist on the illegality of Junot's threats, we denounce his talk about "breaking the contract of employment". We won't give in.

The endless purring of the duplicator.

We move like somnambulists toward daybreak on Thursday. Christian's lined face and feverish eyes frighten me. "Have a rest, we'll look after the leaflets and the hand-out." He doesn't want to. But when he speaks he's choked with coughing. Early Thursday morning Georges arrives without having shaved, the start of a black beard encroaching on his face, and I think Primo's overcoat is creased ... Unthinkable! This week has been lasting forever, when will it end?

Thursday passes in a fog of tiredness, worn nerves, mechanically repeated acts. Hold out for a few more hours. It's the last day of confrontation in the week. Nothing will happen on Friday: departure for everyone at 4:15 p.m., the management enforces no recuperation.

All day Junot goes on with his planing operation.

Our leaflets continue to circulate.

Thursday, five o'clock: just over two hundred strikers.

Our strike has held out all week.

This Friday is February 21st. Every year we commemorate, in an international day of anti-imperialist solidarity, the anniversary of the execution by the Nazis of the Manouchian group, immigrant resistance workers who came from Armenia, Hungary, Poland. Those men of the red posters, feverish, lined faces, strangers and foreigners, pursued and indomitable, killed on February 21, 1944. Images of yesterday and today with the same immigrant proletariat, unbending in its resistance to destruction. I'm glad that this February 21st doesn't find us in defeat.

Junot has put his threats into action: twenty striking comrades have been expelled from their Citroën hostels. Without warning: in the evening, when they returned from the factory, they found their bags outside the door. "You've got five minutes to beat it," the warden said.

How to find new places for them? We do what we can. Chance lodgings.

Saturday. To sleep.

On Sunday we met again, to prepare the second week of the strike. The general feeling was that it would be impossible to stop production for another week. But the majority of the shop floor committee did not anticipate under any circumstances giving in to the humiliation of the extra three-quarters of an hour and especially to the unpaid work. These men had made it into a personal question: nothing would make them change their minds. So we would go on. Even if the numbers of strikers became further eroded. Even if Junot put his other threats into practice. Even if the CFT attacked in force. We would go on for the sake of principle. We would go on because it was really a question of honor, which is not only a word which sounds good in the leaflets. And since a strike, even a minority one, can never be a mere absence from work, it's always a means of resistance, an increase of activity in relation to the work (it's like holding a block of granite: if you let go completely, you're crushed), we brace ourselves again for Monday: new leaflets, a new campaign of explanations. We'll put it into operation at once: this very evening we'll go and visit the strikers we know in their own homes, and in groups of two we'll go around to the hostels—as far as access to them is possible.

On Monday evening, despite our propaganda efforts of the day before, despite the leaflets given out in the morning, despite the discussions in the cloakrooms and during the breaks, the number of strikers fell sharply, by half. Only a hundred or so workers walked out at five o'clock. And, for the first time since the start of the strike, the management succeeded in filling the gaps in the lines and, thanks to replacements by the adjustors, the senior staff, and a few craftsmen, carried on production until a quarter to six, the official end of the day.

Tuesday, February 25th. Five to seven. The morning wait. I walk quickly toward the gantry crane. Yard, main doorway, corridors, iron staircases, right angles, alleyways. Routine itinerary, which I follow without seeing, my thoughts elsewhere. To enter the works is to enter the strike. Beneath my jacket is the packet of leaflets that I'll give to Simon in a few moments, so that he can distribute them along the main assembly line. A full day is in preparation. During the 8:15 break I'll go to number 86 to talk to Mouloud, if Gravier's not in sight. At half-past twelve I'm to meet Mohamed and Primo in the canteen: to check on the paint shop. Oh yes, there is the Malian who said last night that there were some men in the pressing shop who wanted to discuss things. Mustn't forget to go there.

My place. Dupré's waiting for me there. He looks sly. Walking with my head down I almost bumped into him. What the hell's he doing there by the crane?

"You're transferred to the annex in the rue Nationale. Here's your exit pass. You've got to be there at half-past seven."

"But ..."

"There's no but: you've just got time to get there. You must take your clothes with you, you won't be coming back here."

And the leaflets, and my appointments, and the Malian in the pressing shop, and ...

"Well, are you deaf or something? Don't you know the way out?"

The charge hand's getting impatient. I start moving

away hesitantly. I look helplessly at Simon, who's been following the scene from a distance. Impossible to pass him the leaflets, Dupré doesn't take his eyes off me. I'm furious at having them there, under my jacket, a pile of paper that's now useless. I leave the shop. The cloakroom's empty: I change under the eyes of the caretaker. The factory door. Another caretaker: I show my pass, he nods and signs to me with a flabby hand that I can go.

The street. A short walk. Here's the rue Nationale. I look for the address shown.

The store for Panhard spare parts, connected for administrative purposes to the Porte de Choisy Citroën works, stagnates in an old warehouse squeezed into a recess between apartment blocks, a totally isolated cul-de-sac five minutes' walk from the factory. Eleven people work here, including a charge hand and an old guard who's half-deaf.

The ant who's busy in the ant-heap doesn't know that within a few moments a giant hand will remove it carefully from the mass of its companions and set it down far away from everything, in a glass jar. All it can do now is go around and around over the glass walls, still quivering from the recent crowd, stunned by the surprise of its solitude.

While I hurried toward the crane this morning, the packet of leaflets pressed against my body, my head full of things to do with the strike, moving toward the day as one moves toward a battle, my case had already been settled up there in the offices and I didn't know.

Now, it's half-past seven in the morning and I'm in the warehouse, my new place of work. I repeat, stupefied by the rapidity of this change: the works, shop 85, the big assembly line, the 2 CVs, the strike, all that's over for me, I'll only be able to follow it now from outside. But I don't succeed in thinking it.

I'm in the glass jar.

5

Citroën order

The Panhard depot, my place of exile, is about half a mile from the works, buried in the alleyways of the thirteenth arrondissement, away from the open streets where the principal buildings stand, in the Avenue de Choisy and on the main boulevards. This faraway annex owes its origins to the successive strata of the capitalist concentration.

The factories at the Porte de Choisy once belonged to the firm of Panhard. In them they made cars and also well-known armored cars: the Panhard, a small, light, armored weapon for antiguerilla patrols, had been a great success for years during the colonial wars all over the world: involved in how many punitive raids, burned mechtas and villages, civilian crowds gunned down? Today the armored cars are made elsewhere, the firm of Panhard has disappeared, and on the assembly line at the Porte de Choisy, 2 CVs have replaced the armored cars. But Citroën, when buying Panhard and its premises, took over the after-sales service of the defunct firm for a certain period. So they stored in the little rue Nationale warehouse a whole odd collection of spare parts for Panhard cars. We manage this legacy.

From an administrative point of view we belong to Citroën-Choisy. We clock in like the others, are subject to the same hours, under the direction of the same section manager. But we produce nothing. We live in the midst of hundreds of racks spaced out along narrow corridors, where the spare parts are kept, in accordance with a complex numbering system—rather like those spectacular rooms full of records and filing systems that you sometimes see at the cinema, in films about spies or the police. Our work is of deadly simplicity. Taking an order from the charge hand (he has a small pile of them and shares them out among us) and locating what is written on it. To do this we use a cart and go off to get our supplies down alleyways as though we were doing our shopping in a supermarket. When the different objects ordered are assembled we take everything back to the charge hand, who will check them and send them on to the packing department; we take another order and an empty cart and start again. The journeys, which are all the same, down similar alleyways, are equivalent to covering many miles—while the area of the warehouse is in fact ridiculously small. All this in a kind of semidarkness, since the store is only lit by a few weak lightbulbs.

There is also the silence, grating and poor in quality, the scraping of the carts and the gliding of footsteps: everyone drags his feet. And a strong smell of rancid grease which at first gets you by the throat, then finally drugs you—all the spare parts are protected from rust by a thick coating of a brown, sticky substance, oil-based, which I take real pleasure in scraping off with a steel blade when no one's watching me. The sole element of variety is introduced by the exoticism of certain orders: a pinion for Conakry, a gearbox for Abidjan, an axle for São Paulo, you can start dreaming.

Everyone carries out his order as slowly as possible and toward midday the spectacle of these shadows wandering in silence along the dark racks, apparently prey to an incurable lethargy, has something of unreality about it.

I picked up the habit of going off, between two orders, to doze for a few minutes in one of the big racks at the back of the warehouse. Sometimes, crouching down between two engines, I would even succeed in reading one or two pages of a book with a pocket flashlight, forgetting Citroën, Panhard, and the rest of the universe. Sometimes I went right off to sleep and was only wakened by the boss who was worried about my disappearance and went down the alleyways shouting my name. The smell of grease would take hold of me at once and I would start off again to do my "shopping".

Apart from me there were only old men there, whom Citroën had "parked" while they waited for their retirement. We had hardly any common ground for discussion, and in any case the frozen atmosphere of this huge warehouse did not encourage communication. After one week I knew the eleven faces by heart and I realized there was nothing to be done.

Only one old worker would sometimes speak to me. His face, furrowed with wrinkles, seemed to converge toward a drooping, bitter mouth which sometimes smiled in a vague grimace. A thin body, lost in a gray cotton overall pulled in at the waist by a twisted belt. Albert had only one really important occupation left to him: counting the days which separated him from retirement. And in fact he hardly talked to me about anything else, dreaming aloud of an idyllic future in a suburban bungalow, geraniums, little symmetrical gardens, and silent mornings. He passed his time in proving to me with many calculations the ingenious system whereby an accumulation of paid holidays and exceptional gratuities was allowing him to retire at the age of only sixty-four and six months. "It's more or less normal," he would add as though to excuse himself for having this privilege, "in thirty-three years' work with Citroën I've never drawn insurance. No, no, never ill!" Only two months to go: he could see the end.

His other subject of enthusiasm was his son, who'd become a policeman. "You understand, he never touches anything with his hands. He works in white gloves. In the evening, when he sits down to table, he doesn't even need to wash his hands!"

Everything separated me from Albert and yet I had the impression I understood him. The minute breath of life in those uneventful days at the Panhard store.

A few months later, after I had left the store some time before, I met someone who works there by chance:

"Well, how are things in the rue Nationale?"

"Still the same."

"And what about old Albert? Did he retire?"

"Oh, didn't you know? Yes, he retired. And just a month later he died. A heart attack, apparently ..."

Fleeting image: an elderly bird who has always lived in a cage. One day they finally set him free. He thinks he can fly, as though intoxicated, toward liberty. But he doesn't know how to any more. It's too strong, too new. His atrophied wings can't raise him any more. He falls like a dead weight and dies in silence, just in front of the door of his cage which is open at last.

Albert's body had been programmed for sixty-five years of life by those who had used it. Thirty-three years in the Citroën machine: the same alarm clock at the same time every morning, except for the holiday periods, which were always the same. Never ill, never "on insurance", he would say. But a little more used-up each day. And the astonishment of coming to the end of the race: the silence of the alarm clock which will never go off again, the bewilderment of this everlasting idleness ... It was too much.

For me this spare parts warehouse was only a place of restraint. I spent more than a month there. Having sworn that I would not give my notice under any circumstances I'd made myself a prisoner of Citroën. During the first days in the rue Nationale the absurdity of my isolation, while I knew what battle was going on at Choisy at the same time, filled me with a rage for which there was no possible outlet. What the hell was I doing, groping in a dusty rack for a clutch to send to Tartempion-les-Bains, while once again, in number 85, in the paint shop, in Gravier's department, facing Junot and his gang, Primo, Georges, Christian, and all the guys from the committee were getting ready for the five o'clock confrontation. But you can't explain that to an old guard who's half-deaf, to a decrepit charge hand who hasn't seen an assembly line for ten years, or to an old worker who's obsessed by the approach of his retirement!

It's current practice, in large firms, to relegate troublemakers, restless people, or overtiresome militant trade unionists to isolated places, remote annexes, shops, courses, or stores. Punishment always entails the risk of provoking a row and mobilizing people around the victim. Why run this risk if you can obtain the same result without possible appeal? The bosses are the only masters in the organization of work, aren't they? If the management decides that you're indispensable for the supervision of a lumberroom, a good half mile away from the workshop where you were implanted, you can only comply or give notice.

I knew that. But I hadn't imagined the severe shock that it represents. You feel torn out, like a live limb cut away from the organism, still throbbing. During the first days I missed the familiar universe of the main assembly line and its dependencies. I missed everything. Simon's rapid journeys back and forth as he pushed his carts and carried the leaflets. The little friendly gestures from the Yugoslavs at the roundabout. The women in the upholstery shop. The slow, dignified walk of the Malians. Christian's burst of anger, Sadok's furtive visits, the little meetings on the third step ... Everything.

For ten hours a day I was shut up in a ridiculous cul-de-sac, reduced to counting the hours and anxiously calculating the effect of our strike. At five o'clock in the evening, one second after clocking out, I would run off without even going through the cloakroom, and arrive a few minutes later, breathless, at the Choisy gates, to get news of the factory, this world which had become suddenly remote, and was forbidden to me.

The news was bad.

First of all the continued erosion of the strike. Then, after a brief apparent respite, the disbanding of the shopfloor committee.

At the end of the second week of the strike, the situation had settled down. Fifty or so workers at the Choisy factory continued to reject recuperation and walked out every evening at five o'clock. Scattered throughout the workshops, on the lines, on piece-work or in laboring jobs, they were now going out individually without hope of stopping production. Their obstinacy, concentrated into this gesture which had now become symbolic, proved every day the existence of a last resistance group to the humiliation of the extra three-quarters of an hour.

In this last group there were workers whom we didn't know, who had never been to the committee meetings, to whom we had never had occasion to speak in the factory.

Conversely, in the end certain members of the committee had given up the daily stoppage.

The majority of the committee members continued to reject recuperation and went home at five o'clock. But an implicit consensus had been established, leaving each man the individual choice of this act. Simon, Sadok, and some of the Malians decided to give up at the end of the second week and submit to the management's work schedules. Although nobody asked them to do so, each explained his reasons, which were due to personal difficulties or to particular means of pressure which the Citroën management could apply to them. Everyone felt their confusion and to what extent this abandonment was painful for them. The others did not blame them for it. We knew that the strike proper, as a collective action, was in fact over, having been progressively limited, planed away, and reduced by the management. We wouldn't cause it to start again. Those who were going on were only keeping to a promise they had entered into with themselves. Primo had sworn he wouldn't give in: no change of tactics would have made him change his mind. The same was true of Georges, Stepan, Pavel, Christian, and a few others.

For a few days it looked as though this situation would continue.

At five o'clock the fifty recalcitrant workers went to the cloakrooms without incident. Their posts had been known for a long time and the adjustors proceeded immediately to replace them on the lines. For the posts on piece-work and the laborers' jobs, absences of three-quarters of an hour had hardly any immediate effect on production.

Order appeared to have returned, production was normally assured during the ten hours of the working day: I imagined that the Citroën system would lose interest in the symbolic demonstration represented by the departure of fifty men at five o'clock. But I didn't know the system well enough. Are the workers devoted to symbols? So are the bosses. To make people produce is not enough. They must be made to submit. Put more exactly, as far as the management is concerned the producers must submit to ensure a certain amount of production: the slightest threat that they will assert themselves again is intolerable, even if there is hardly any immediate material consequence. The system neglects nothing.

Suddenly, at the beginning of March, with no prior announcement, the management began a systematic persecution of the most active workers from the shop floor committee. This selective repression was aimed with such precision at the hard-core elements in our group that I wondered how far the Citroën police spy system had allowed them to get to know our internal functioning.

They fell in succession: Christian, Georges, Stepan, Pavel, Primo.

The method of attack was the same in each case. No firing, but intensive erosion; making life impossible for the man in question. The entire system of supervision, harassment, and blackmail which had come into action from February 18th against all the striking workers in the factory was now concentrated, methodically, on the known "hardliners". The management had chosen a mere ten or so persons to be eliminated. They would know how to make them "give notice"—and disappear.

Christian.

Dupré spent a week tormenting him. He forbade him to move anywhere in the shop. The Breton, a highly nervous man, had a vital need of action and movement and he only found a certain stability in leaving his rack every two or three hours to take a walk around the shop. This enforced stillness was a severe shock for him. Christian gritted his teeth and held out for two or three days. But he became more irritable, losing composure over details, speaking sharply to neighbors.

Then Dupré began to annoy him about his way of arranging the pieces of rubber. He made him re-do a seat which was supposed to be irregular. Then another. Then he triumphantly informed him one Thursday at five o'clock that the minimum output was increased by five seats and that if he didn't stay to do them a sum would be deducted from his pay. Wild with rage, Christian threw a piece of rubber in the direction of Dupré—without hitting him—and yelled that he was giving in his notice. The other man couldn't have asked for more. He accompanied him to the office without a word, didn't even mention the violent action, and handed him over to the section manager who made him sign his resignation papers. Less than a quarter of an hour later he was outside the door, stunned by his own outbreak and by this sudden departure. Citroën was over for him.

On my arrival from the rue Nationale I found him there, quivering with indignation, desperately upset that they had got him.

"I've been stupid. My nerves gave way ..."

Georges, Stepan, Pavel.

The three Yugoslavs from the roundabout had organized their work a long time ago, independently of official arrangements. Allocated to the assembly of the locks, they had transformed and regrouped the operations in order to free themselves in rotation from the slavery of the assembly line. Their manual skill and speed had allowed them in this way to take over an area of autonomous functioning in a section where only the decisions of the work-study office were supposed to prevail. The senior staff, who found only advantages in this arrangement—there was never any delay or any defective part—left them alone.

When the decision to get at them was taken, the foreman Huguet had no difficulty in finding the most effective means of reprisal against the three men: he separated them. One fine morning this little corner of Yugoslavia installed over the ten yards of the three roundabout posts was shattered. Three transfers. Pavel found himself in the pressing shop, Stepan in the paint shop, and Georges in the sanding shop (a post that was hated, because it forced you to remain ten hours a day in the midst of iron dust and a whirlwind of minute fragments of metal).

Dispersed and brutally deprived of a rhythm in their working life that they'd built up patiently over the years, allocated to jobs which were especially unpleasant, the three Yugoslavs decided by common agreement that that was enough.

The three of them gave notice the same morning.

They left their posts without a glance at the bosses, who were hanging about them, announced their decision to the office, and allowed their papers to be prepared in silence. But, before going out, they made a complete round of the different workshops to speak for a last time to all the workers they knew, and all those who had taken part in the walk-outs, and all the members of the shop floor committee. They shook hands with everyone. They themselves were already in their outdoor clothes and they shook all the hands covered with dirty grease, oil, metal dust, paint, but they shook them at length, with words of farewell and encouragement. The others stopped working for a few moments, put down their tools, thanked them for all they had done, and wished them luck for the future. That took a long time, but no charge hand, no foreman, no guard dared make the slightest remark or try to accelerate the action. It was only after visiting the entire works in this way, even its most remote corners, that they left through the main door, brushing against the guard without taking any more notice of him than if he'd been a utensil forgotten there by chance.

Finally came Primo's turn.

It was harder with the Sicilian, who was quite determined not to hand in his notice.

It began by the usual method of harassment over work: paintwork to be redone, this coat's too thick, this coat's too thin, etc. No success: Primo complied, impassive.

Then came transfers: he was dragged to the stamping shop, then the sanding. In two weeks he did five or six different jobs, was used as a stopgap and taken away from his work as soon as he began to get used to it.

In the end the management decided to take extreme measures. An *agent provocateur* from the CFT came to insult him while he was working, telling him sharply that the shop floor committee men were only layabouts and that if they refused to work until a quarter to six it was only due to laziness, that in any case immigrant workers were useless and that he, a "dirty Ita" Primo's punch cut the man's cheek right open. Two stitches.

And for Primo, immediate dismissal.

Further, Citroën took legal action against the Sicilian: "grievous bodily harm."

The decapitated shop floor committee became dormant.

People continued to say "the committee men" when they talked about one or another of us (and we still used this expression ourselves), but the Friday meetings stopped, as well as the hand-out of leaflets.

Abandoned by the outgoing tide in my small puddle in the rue Nationale, I continued feebly piling up my Panhard spare parts, and whenever I was forgotten for a few minutes I would doze off at the back of the warehouse. The management left me to stagnate there, waiting for me to give notice. But as I had decided I would not go voluntarily under any circumstances, I settled down to wait, melancholy and as though frozen. The first days of spring 1969 were in fact cold, and I curled up within myself, counting the last days of this March which had lost its savor, trying to read novels in the darkness of the giant racks, scraping off with a razorblade the thick, solid grease which covered the pinions or the engines, listening vaguely to Albert's senile dreams.

Isolation, the absence of any precise object on which I could concentrate my anger (I had no cause for any grudge against the wormeaten charge hand, nor to attack the guard, who dozed by the time clock), the repeated going over in my mind of the repression at Choisy—which here became abstract—finally exhausted the anger I had felt at the start. I had progressively adopted the same dragging step as my colleagues, and sometimes, as I glided in the silence of the warehouse in search of some gear lever or a windshield, I felt invisible slippers on my feet.

News would reach me, through chance meetings and the incidental comings and goings between the rue Nationale and the Avenue de Choisy.

Pavel had found work again almost immediately in a printing shop.

Georges succeeded in being taken on by Renault at Billancourt. He would come to see me sometimes, still free and easy, laughing at my exile and my melancholy, urging me to give notice: "Chuck it in. For the next holidays come with me to Yugoslavia. I'll introduce everyone in my village to you. We'll have a good time. There are beautiful girls up there." And without any further transition he began to recount his amorous exploits.

Stepan remained unemployed for a long time and finally left for West Germany.

I was anxious about Christian, who was said to be desperate and who, on another impulse, had gone back to Brittany, where all the same he knew he would not be able to find work or count on anyone, his family being much too poor to keep him for long. His girlfriend from the lycée was looking for him everywhere, in vain.

Those who had survived and kept their jobs at Choisy—Simon, Sadok, Mohamed from the paint shop, and a few others—were dejected and waiting for better days. The forthcoming closure of the Choisy works, announced for the following year, increased everyone's uncertainty about his own fate. Who would be transferred to Javel? to Levallois? to Clichy? to the provinces? Hadn't they suggested to young panel beaters that they should leave for ... Brussels! The restoration of order had driven each man back into his solitude. When I happened to meet Sadok in the evening and we exchanged a few words I found his speech was slurred and his breath smelled strongly of alcohol.

The only one with whom I maintained regular contact was Primo. He had found a job in a precision instruments firm, near the Place d'Italie. A very small place, where there were no more than twenty or so workers.

We formed the habit of meeting every Friday. Primo finished later than I did. So I would set off on foot to meet him as he came out of his firm. He would appear, punctually, upright in his black overcoat. We would go to have a cup of coffee in a big saloon in the Place d'Italie. Sometimes, afterward, I would take him back to my place for supper. These meetings would take place in accordance with a ritual that was always identical. First of all I would give him newspapers and brochures, I would reply to his questions about the state of things in our section (What was happening about the strike of loaders at the Austerlitz post office? And the charwomen, employed by a firm of sub-contractors to the SNCF, who were almost taking the skin off their hands while cleaning the refrigerated railway cars at the Masséna warehouse, practically without any tools, were they soon going to start the action that had been planned? And the garbage men at Ivry? And the victims of the intensive building program who'd been left homeless?). Then we would talk about the other Citroën plants, about France, about the world. Then we would talk about just anything. On my side, once I had made the effort to give the political exposé, and after Primo had given me his opinion and passed on whatever news he had, I would remain almost silent, returning very quickly to my lethargy. Primo realized I was remote and he would try to raise my morale.

I would listen to him vaguely, as if through a fog.

Interminable winter.

One evening.

I've emerged more dejected than usual from my ridiculous work at the warehouse in the rue Nationale. Nothing's happened since Monday. I haven't even exchanged more than a few sentences with Albert. I haven't even read two pages of a novel. I've piled up my Panhard spare parts, I've eaten, I've slept. I've had no news of Choisy, nor of anyone. I don't know what I'm doing there any more, nor what I'm waiting for. It's a Friday: automatically I go toward Primo's firm, although I've even forgotten to bring the newspapers which I was due to give him.

The saloon. Glittering, noisy. Smooth surfaces, reflections, clouds of smoke, pooltable, jukebox. Primo talks to me. I listen to him a little, and I also listen to the song coming from the jukebox (I find the girl singer's voice beautiful and sensual, and I find myself overcome by a sudden, unexplained nostalgia). We've gone to sit in a corner, I on a chair and Primo on the end of a bench covered in American cloth. All at once I catch sight of myself in the vast mirror facing me, behind Primo. I look so crushed, my head sunk into my shapeless overcoat, a leather hat pulled down over my eyes, that I half-smile in derison.

Primo has stopped talking.

He shakes me by the elbow.

Then he says to me, in a soft, suddenly different voice (and at once I begin to listen to him, and I forget the jukebox song and the sounds of the saloon):

"You know, our strike's not a failure. It's not a failure because ..."

He stops there, searching for words.

"... because we're all glad to have done it. All of us. Yes, even those who were forced to go and those who've been transferred were glad to have done it. The Choisy workers whom I meet say that the bosses are more careful now.

There are fewer rows. The speed of output hasn't been increased since the strike. The management's taken the strike seriously, like a warning. It'll be remembered a long time, you know. They even talk about it in the other Citroën plants. The Choisy men now say: 'We at Choisy have shown that we don't let people do what they like with us.' This strike is the proof that you can fight in the toughest places. There'll be others, you'll see ..."

He said: "... in the toughest places ... you'll see ..."

I think, as I listen to him, that I like his accent and this strength which keeps him rigid, unconquered. I think of Sicily and the proletarians who've come as far as this from the scorched lands of the south. I feel a little less cold, but I remain sceptical.

And yet he's right.

Months later, and years later, I will meet by chance former workers from Choisy who will all talk to me about the strike and the committee, and will tell me how far the memory of it has remained alive, at Javel, at Levallois, at Clichy, along the vast assembly lines for the DS and in the unbearable heat of the foundries, in the nauseating vapors of the paint shops, and in the crackling sparks in the soldering shops, in all the places where, once our factory was closed, they transferred its workers. Other strikes, other committees, other actions will take their inspiration from earlier strikes—and from ours, of which I shall find traces later, mingled with those of so many others ...

Primo is right, but at the moment that he's talking to me I don't realize it yet, because I'm preoccupied with chewing over the impotence of my exile and the crushing re-establishment of the Citroën order.

6

World opinion

One morning, just as suddenly as I had received my order to go into exile, I was informed of my return to Choisy.

"You've got half an hour to get to the works. Here now, there's your pass."

Cloakroom. Streets. The Avenue de Choisy, in fine rain, deserted at this early morning hour. The main door of the factory. That's it, I'm going to find the familiar crowd in the workshops again. The guard throws a dejected glance at my pass, lets me in. I think that within a few moments I'll be with friends.

No question of it.

The section manager Junot places me at the disposal of the foreman Gravier, who puts me at the disposal of the adjustor Danglois. Still the hierarchic order, the "Follow me", the "Wait there", the "Put it there" ... When you put a worker in one place, you never miss this opportunity for putting him in *his* place. It's a practice which is applied to everyone, which is part of the normal functioning of the firm. In my case, however, they seem to be especially unpleasant: the orders are really barked out. The strike has no doubt earned me this tougher treatment (I shall soon know that they are now aware of my "establishment" status).

The adjustor Danglois, under whom I now work, is a fat man with puffy, weak features. He's rigged up in a gray coat that he puts on "to look like a boss". But he draws his real status in the place from elsewhere: he's a member of the CFT office. This post of responsibility in the "yellow" union assures him of an obvious complement of power: the charge hands and the foremen speak to him as an equal. The senior staff show him a familiarity and a consideration that the general run of adjustors do not receive. He takes advantage of it freely, always anxious to show himself in close company with people more powerful than himself. Moreover, he's a crafty, lazy, cowardly man, ineffective in his work (in fact he spends his day hanging about here and there), ready to threaten the workers, always obsequious when a senior person in the Citroën hierarchy appears. I think that behind their familiarity toward him even the foremen despise him. But they're on guard: the CFT hierarchy duplicates the Citroën hierarchy, completing it with its autonomous circuit of denouncement and black-mail. A man like Danglois can be formidable, even to the executive staff.

My new post, then. Danglois explains it to me rapidly, with the ironic condescension that can be caused by such a subordinate task.

Strange work, which owes its existence only to the archaic nature of the place. Here's the reason for it: the arrangement of the buildings, which are separated by a yard, causes discontinuity in the process of assembling the 2 CVs; my job is to operate the junction, to ensure the continuity of the assembly. In fact I replace, on my own, a section of the line!

This is how things are.

When you look at the plant from the yard, you see two compact blocks of buildings, one on the left, the other on the right, linked on their first and second floors but divided at ground level by the front part of the yard and the stock area.

The left-hand block includes: on the ground floor, the pressing shop; on the first floor, the shop with the main assembly line, number 85; on the second floor, part of the paint shop which also extends over the second floor of the right-hand block.

The right-hand block includes: on the ground floor, a

stock area; on the mezzanine floor, slightly below the level of the first floor, the soldering shop, number 86; on the second floor, the paint shop.

Now the assembly process.

Delivery trucks, coming from other, sometimes distant, plants, deposit containers, engines, and sections of sheet metal, either molded or in thin sheets, in the yard and the various stock areas. The principal components of the body skeleton, the doors, fenders, etc., arrive in sections which are already assembled.

In the pressing shop a few supplementary parts are pressed out and a preliminary assembly of the whole thing takes place. From here there emerges a kind of sheet-metal body, unsteady and looking as though it's patched up all over, but the shape is already recognizable as a 2 CV. It's the "shell".

This "shell", accompanied by the doors and fenders (which remain separated until the assembly on the big line in number 85), goes off to the soldering shop, Gravier's area, where obvious cracks and nailmarks will be removed, giving the whole coachwork an impression of unity. I've already described this semicircle of thirty or so work positions situated on the mezzanine floor, its grayness and iron dust, its smell of burning, and its sprays of silvery sparks—my first post with Citroën.

After the soldering shop the shell, swallowed by a moving tunnel, goes off to the paint shop (chemical coatings, the paint sprayers succeeding each other in the clouds of vapors, corrosive acids, varnishes ...), then it comes down on a hoist to the main assembly line, where the engine is fixed on the chassis and the interior fittings are added (upholstery, windows, linings, wheels, dashboards, etc.).

Then comes the finishing, the last checks, the trying out, the car removed by a "trainer" who takes the steering wheel and parks the car temporarily while waiting for it to be loaded onto a tractor-trailer which will take it off to its destiny as merchanidise: for sale.

The plant spits out a finished car every four minutes.

All transfers from one shop to another are carried out by machines (bridges, moving tunnels, lines at ground level or overhead, hoists), except for the passage of the shells from embossing to soldering. This is where I come in: my new post is between the two first stages of the assembly. Since there is no physical link between embossing and soldering—the two shops belong respectively to the left and right blocks and are separated by the front part of the yard—someone has to take the nailed-up shell and transport it a distance of three hundred feet across the yard, until it's beneath the soldering shop, from where the hoist operator brings it up to the mezzanine floor.

This transporting of the shells is done on metal carts: low, heavy, and on little wheels, they stick hard to the asphalt of the yard and when you move them they creak and groan.

So on these carts I shall have about a hundred and fifty shells to transport every day. I have to stack up the carts which have arrived and been unloaded: then take them back to where they started from, the exit from the pressing shop, five at a time. A hundred and fifty shells to bring over, thirty-times-five iron carts to take back. This is the hardest part: there must be more than a hundred kilos on each trip. Later, but only once, I try to divide up the return journey; but I soon realize that is a mistake: the carts are so low that if you push an empty one, or just two, piled one on top of the other, you're walking bent double, almost on all fours, and in the end the position becomes intolerable: it's better to stack up the five and hold on about three feet above the ground—you're pulling along their hundred kilos of cast iron and more, but at least you can stand more or less upright.

All that in a yard completely open to the wind and rain, often slippery, cluttered with trucks, trailers, and containers. And only having for company, almost permanently, the adjustor Danglois, urging me to go faster.

No, there's no question of mingling again with my work-mates in the shops.

After restraint, forced labor.

Danglois has finished his explanations. In order to watch me start he's posted himself a few yards away from my departure point, near the sliding door to the pressing shop, from where the repeated din of the presses can be clearly heard. Instinctively the adjustor has assumed the traditional stance of the jailer, legs apart, hands on hips. The belt of his gray coat, loosely tied in a sling, emphasizes his caricature-like, near-obscene obesity.

I take a cart, dirty red in color, rattle of metal—the ice-cold cast iron burns my hands. I place the carshell on the cart, somewhat clumsily, trying to find the most suitable hold for this odd assembly of pieces of sheet metal, all patched together. And I start off, braced against my load. Cold contact with the untreated metal—take care not to cut yourself, the edges are sharp and threatening—I stop and come back to ask for some gloves.

Danglois: "There ain't none, get your finger out."

Then, jeeringly: "In any case you're there to take a beating."

No reply possible. The sudden wave of hatred provoked by the overbearing attitude, arrogant stupidity, sure of itself. I'd forgotten a bit. In one sense they do you good, these little unexpected injustices which rap out idiotically without warning. Your pugnacity is aroused. You grit your teeth and await revenge.

I cast a black look at Danglois and go off again to push my cart.

An icy wind. Scudding rain which goes through the light jacket of my blue work clothes. I'm wearing the same clothes I had for my sleepy comings and goings in the warehouse in the rue Nationale. In this yard I feel as though I'm naked, soaked to the skin: the rain, then—after half an hour—sweat. Shall have to think about a tunic, fit myself out. Gloves, too. Tomorrow. Today: blisters and chilblains.

This heavy laboring work, exhausting and exposed to bad weather, is one of the most unpleasant jobs in the works. What's more, Danglois and, from time to time, Gravier come to scorn me and provoke me. Danglois pretends to be afraid of an interruption to the assembly work ("Oh, only four shells ahead? That won't do! Get some guts into it!"). Gravier, the foreman, amuses himself by coming to time me every now and then, snidely remarking to me in a sibilant voice: "You're patient, but we're more patient than you." (He's begun to address me as *vous* since he learned that I'm a "university type" by origin, and not a worker.)

Citroën is really laying it on with a trowel to make me hand in my notice. But the opposite occurs. After three weeks of this regime I've lost about five pounds but I've got back a good part of my morale. I've sworn I wouldn't go, I've just got to stand up to them. I treat Danglois with irony, Gravier with silence. During the breaks I find Sadok and Mouloud again, along with a few workmates from the soldering shop that I'd lost sight of. The drivers, as they go by, come to discuss things. In the canteen I make contact again with the men from the committee, with my workmates from the shop on the main assembly line, with Mohamed the Kabylian, and the paint shop men. Even Jojo, the old CGT member, my former neighbor in the cloakroom, is still there, and glad to see me. The impression of cataclysm that I'd felt when our strike was suddenly crushed, when I was exiled to the rue Nationale, and the shop floor committee lost its most active elements as they were forced to give notice, this impression fades now like a wound that's healing. Everything remains in its place. They and us. They, still just as immediately detestable (I've found them again now, I'm on the lookout, I hold on, sweating, my back painful, my hands bruised, gritting my teeth beneath the coarse jokes), we are indefinably renewed but perpetually having to find ways to resist the outbreaks of bad temper, the shouts of rage at a minute stolen from break, the inexplicable slowing-down of the line, and the accidents on a Friday, when a hook suddenly twists and blocks the machinery in the midst of bursts of laughter and pieces of rubber that fly in all directions; we make our plans in the canteen, where newspapers and leaflets circulate; we have news to exchange, we have the shared sandwich and the offered cigarette, and the gesture of help and comfort when we're near collapse; and there we are, speaking all languages, coming from all countries, collected together, scattered, separated, brought together again, always apart and always near. I've not been into the workshops again, but I feel them very near, and news reaches me, so that my anger mingles with that of the others. And even my hate for Danglois, Gravier, and those who give them their orders, I feel it like a feeling of belonging. A class feeling.

Try if you can to forget the class struggle when you're a factory worker! The boss doesn't forget it and you can count on him to remind you of it!

When I'd counted my hundred and fifty 2 CVs and my day as a one-man assembly line was over, I would go home and collapse in a heap. I no longer had the strength to think about much, but at least I was giving a precise content to the concept of added value.

The meeting with Ali played a decisive role in the transformation of my state of mind. A shock, but one so complex that even today I couldn't define it precisely, now that nearly ten years have passed. A breath of air from the great outside, the sudden vision of masses so much more distant and more obscure, and also the discovery of something fraternal and tragic at the same time. But words, suddenly, seem feeble to me, and inappropriate.

I only knew Ali for a single day.

A complete working day, from seven o'clock in the morning until five o'clock in the evening.

And, although I've never seen him since, I often think of him.

That morning my work as a one-man assembly line was embellished with a variant.

There had been an incident in the pressing shop. Several presses were working unevenly, and although all the tooling workers and electricians were at their posts, production was irregular for the moment: the car shells were going out intermittently. The routine of my forward and backward journeys and the continuous supply to the soldering shop were therefore in danger. But this type of interruption was anticipated and a complementary arrangement went into operation.

On my arrival, at seven o'clock, Danglois takes me into a huge building, isolated at the far end of the yard, where several hundred 2 CV shells are piled in rows. It's a reserve. There's a man there, standing in the middle of a row. Danglois indicates him to me with a casual flick of his thumb: "He'll pass you shells whenever there's a shortage from the pressing shop; you'll only have to go through here to fill up. Get it?" I nod my head vaguely. The man has not moved. He seems not even to have heard. Danglois urges me to start my circuit. We go out together. I turn rapidly toward the pressing shop.

Start. Shells. A heap of carts. Shells. The circuit now known by heart, down to the smallest defect in the asphalt, the imaginary figures and the badly formed letters that I think I can read in the unevenness of the ground, the usual traffic blocks in the yard, the rumble of wheels, these routine sounds that sink into your head and your muscles until they become gradually a stranger-like part of yourself—and then you need a certain amount of time to rid yourself of this absurd routine. Shell. Carts. A gap. The pressing shop's falling behind. Go to the building with the stock. The man hands me a shell, prepares another one. Quickly, to the place below the end of the soldering shop. The man on the hoist's getting impatient: he shouts to me to hurry. I can see the charge hand up there beside him, urging him to go faster. Quick, back to the stock building. Take the shell away (the man's already preparing a third one). The man on the hoist. Go back to the embossing shop. Still no shell. The stock building. A shell. There are no more iron carts. Get them back from the place below the soldering shop and make a pile of five. Take them all back to the stock place. Take another shell. Faster, shouts the hoist man, perpetually spurred on by the charge hand in the soldering shop. Another. Go and see what's happening in the pressing shop. It's working again. Shells are starting to pile up untidily in front of the shop door, blocking the way. A fork lift can't move: the driver calls to me to make room for it. I move two or three shells and begin to take my stock from here again. Shells. Carts back. Run along the ritual circuit, because I'm late. New stoppage in pressing. Run to the stock building. The man passes me a shell ...

Each time I go past the warehouse I throw him a rapid look, sometimes a smile, but without ever having the time to stop or speak to him. He, on his side, never says a word.

He's tall, very thin, with a brown skin. I seem to know him by sight, having noticed, when passing him in the shops or the cloakrooms, the blue tattoo mark, in the form of a dot between his eyebrows, which emphasizes his look. As soon as I enter the building he hands me a shell, which he carries in his arms, keeping them wide apart, with a regular, precise movement, always identical. Then he assumes his pose again at once: motionless, right in the middle of the warehouse, his arms folded, his expression distant, as though he were standing guard at some desert camp.

I've often thought of talking to him, but I'm too rushed, running all over the yard with my wobbling car shells and my cast iron carts. And since he himself appears to be so remote, the maneuver is repeated in silence.

A quarter past eight: ten-minute break for a snack. I come to take shelter in the storage warehouse, which is icy but protected from the fine rain which continues to descend on the yard in little squalls. I lean against a carshell and take out my sandwich. The man with the tattoo doesn't move. Still standing, unmoved by the break: it doesn't seem to concern him. I come closer and offer him a share, since he doesn't appear to have brought anything to eat. He glances at the bread, from which protrudes a slice of ham, and shakes his head in refusal:

"I don't eat pig-meat."

Then, in a lower voice, as though he were not speaking directly to me but going on with his reverie:

"I'm the son of a marabout.

"My father is a very important marabout, a great religious man.

"I have studied a good deal.

"Studied Arabic a good deal.

"Arabic grammar.

"It's very important."

A silence. Then he suddenly gazes at me (the surprise of those two sparkling eyes, intensely black) and launches into a long speech, the complete meaning of which I understand with difficulty, because his French is halting, with a rough accent, and because he often seems to me to use one word in place of another—and sometimes even words that are unknown. I understand all the same that his name is Ali, that he's a Moroccan, from a very religious family, that he has studied the Koran, that his father is dead, that his family has been living in poverty for a long time. Then follows the story of a confused personal incident where a knife is mentioned on several occasions, while the general meaning escapes me. He appears to be mingling quotations from the Koran into his story, but I do not grasp their significance either. Then, without transition, he pronounces very distinctly—as though spelling them out in order for me to understand—a few brief sentences. And here I understand again, and what he says makes a strong impression on me:

"The Arabic language is a very great language.

"It was the Arabs who invented grammar.

"They also invented mathematics, and figures for the whole world.

"They have invented many things."

He has raised his voice, and his pride resounds strangely in the metallic warehouse, which sends back an echo.

I feel moved and begin a rather solemn reply, choosing my words in order to say in simple sentences that I have a great respect for Arab culture. And, during the time that I am embarking on this reply, I seem to see us from afar, alone, standing face to face, in this huge and empty building, where there are only piles of car shells, gray pieces of metal, mindless frameworks of cars to come. I with my worn blue cloth jacket, torn by the sharp pieces of iron which catch it. He loosely clad in a laborer's boiler suit which is too wide for his slight build, too short for his great height. And this solemn, unreal dialogue, about the powerful men of remote cultures, remote languages, ways of being remote. And none of this seems to me ridiculous or out of place, but on the contrary serious and important.

The end of break, made real by a bark from Danglois appearing in the framework of the door ("What are you waiting for?"), interrupts my speech in the middle of a sentence. I must start again on my journeys back and forth, leaving Ali standing in the middle of the warehouse, still in the same place.

Ritual circuit for a while, then another stoppage in the pressing shop. I come to take a shell from Ali's stock. Now I have the impression that he's looking at me with sympathy. At least his face appears to me less rigid. I would like to talk, to continue our recent dialogue—but no time. I just say to him as I go by: "O.K.?"—"O.K.", he replies with a slight movement of his lips which can pass for a smile. In fact during the whole day I've never seen him smile more: I thought that Ali was a man who did not smile.

An hour after restarting work the rhythm accelerates further, I'm completely overwhelmed. The pressing shop business has broken my system. Impossible to find a rhythm. The hoist man in Gravier's department becomes irritable, shouts to me to go more quickly, that there are only one or two shells ahead, that there's going to be a gap in the assembly line. If I help myself regularly from the reserve stock warehouse the pressing starts up again unexpectedly and in ten minutes there's a complete pile-up of shells at the shop door—a traffic jam of fork lifts, recriminations from the drivers, Danglois arrives, yelling ...

Then a new stoppage in the pressing shop, a rush to Ali's place, complaints from the hoist man, and so on.

At ten o'clock I'm sweating, out of breath, irritable, and I don't succeed in getting even slightly ahead.

As I go back to the warehouse for a shell Ali says to me: "I'm cold."

Ridiculous situation. The task which has been assigned to him consists only of a few movements every quarter of an hour or so: the rest of the time he freezes on the spot, standing still in this icy warehouse.

Conversely I rush about in all directions, just as heated as he's frozen.

It seems logical to split the difference and we agree to change methods: in the future we will do all the work together, dividing it into two between us. Ali will double up on my circuit with pressing-soldering stock and will transport part of the shells. I will help myself from the piles in the reserve stock warehouse when I'm short of shells. This arrangement will allow Ali to move a little more and me to slow down. Working together we'll get it done very well without rushing.

A short, quiet half hour. This new state of affairs suits us both very well. And then, chaos! Danglois darts out, livid with rage, his thick lower lip twisted (I think he's drooling in fact), his gray coat flapping over his fat with each movement. He shouts at us—at us, and we're very surprised: in fact we've just re-established the advance in the supply of shells, the bosses should be glad:

"What's this? What's this? What the hell's going on here? You do the carts, he does the warehouse."

And turning to Ali:

"You damn well better get back in the warehouse, and don't let me see you in the yard, O.K.?"

Ali shrugs his shoulders slightly, makes me a helpless little sign and returns to the warehouse at a measured pace.

I'd forgotten that I was in the yard as a punishment. This sort of thing counts more than the immediate production of the 2 CVs. Or rather, it's through this sort of thing that

Citroën imagines it will guarantee the long-term production of the 2 CVs. Gravier has sworn to make me hand in my notice: too bad if the assembly line in the soldering shop is permanently threatened by a gap. It's a risk to be taken and it can constitute a reason for punishment, even dismissal (in fact, a few days later they'll clobber me with a warning about insufficient production). So for me it's normal treatment. But Ali? Why has Danglois gone for the Moroccan so violently?

I realize that Ali's post also is a punishment. Since he's tall and strong he's much more affected by this long motionless waiting in the cold than he would be by heavy work. My case is rather the reverse: intense physical effort is very soon hard for me. In fact Gravier and Danglois have succeeded here in what one can call a rational organization of work. These ridiculous arrangements, which are there to show who's in command: the work itself is constructed as a system of repression, only light thumb pressure is needed to reach the limits of what is tolerable.

But why Ali?

I take advantage of a trip to the stock warehouse to ask him. "What have they got against you?"

Ali: "It's because I leave at five o'clock."

So, he belongs to the handful of indomitables who persist in rejecting recuperation, nearly two months after the movement started. Yet I never saw him at the committee meetings, and nobody has ever mentioned him to me.

(I tell myself that Ali has read our leaflet in the Arabic version—I imagine him carefully deciphering for himself the majestic curves and scrolls, which tell him about affront to dignity and strike for the sake of honor—and he must have made his decision without consulting anyone, irrevocably.

I also tell myself that Primo has never met Ali but that when the leaflet was being drawn up he knew how to find the words which would speak to Ali.

And I think that I'm here only temporarily, but in the factories there will always be Primos and Alis).

Noon. Canteen. I don't see Ali there.

The resumption of work at a quarter to one gets off to a promising start: Danglois has disappeared—he's no doubt taken his delegate hours, this carping adjustor who's supposed to represent us in the name of the CFT union. We let a little time go by (perhaps the Calvados is going down slowly?), then, since we don't see him reappearing, we return to our arrangement of the morning. Working together all along the circuit. Sometimes, so that we can talk, we stand side by side behind the same car shell that we push along quietly.

Not always easy, understanding what Ali has to say. Sometimes the words are full of excitement, sometimes they're cut short, the words run together. There are breaks, long silences. On the whole, though, I manage to understand.

All at once Ali begins to talk to me about his life a long time ago. Very poor village in the south of Morocco. Big family, terribly poor. Brothers and sisters dead very young. The French occupation. One memory in particular comes back to him strongly:

"There was a French captain in the village.

"The captain had a big black dog.

"Every week a different family had to feed the big black dog, with meat.

"Everyone was afraid of this week.

"When we fed the dog there was nothing left for feeding anybody: we children were hungry all week.

"Everybody was afraid of the black dog week."

He stops for a moment, steadying the 2 CV car shell that we're pushing. As if the terrors of his childhood were suddenly catching him in the throat. His eyes become misty. He looks elsewhere. It's a shock for me, suddenly seeing, in the adult's angular face, the frightened features of the Moroccan child of the past, the child left hungry forever, the child who will be pursued by the big black dog until he dies. I don't know what to say. I murmur:

"It's terrible ... It's colonialism."

He's recovered and we start pushing again. He makes me this strange reply:

"No, 'colonelism', it's good."

— ?

"'Colonelism', it's good. Colonel Nasser, Colonel Boumedienne. It's good for us."

Our conversation, interrupted by the transport of shells, the maneuver of loading and unloading, the handling of the cast iron carts, dies away, then starts up again, with moments of communication and others of strangeness. A question leaps up again at a memory. Stops at an incomprehensible word.

To something that I say to him or ask him (what was it about? food, or something to smoke, I don't remember), he replied sharply:

"No, I never do that, it's 'Jewish'."

I: "How do you mean, it's 'Jewish'?"

He: "That means: it's not good, you mustn't do it."

I: "But now, 'Jews' are a nationality, a religion."

He: "No, no. 'Jew' is the reverse of other people. You say 'Jewish' when you mean it's not as it should be."

I: "But there's a Jewish language ..."

He: "A Jewish language? No! No!"

I: "But there is, it's called Hebrew."

He: "No, writing 'Jewish' is writing Arabic backwards. It's written in the same way, but the other way around."

I stop.

"Listen, Ali, I know what I'm talking about, I'm Jewish myself."

And he, not put out, with an indulgent shake of his head and almost the ghost of a smile:

"But you can't be Jewish. You are all right. Jewish means when it's not all right."

This could have gone on for hours. Another blockage. The operations of shell-unloading interrupt us again.

The afternoon went by in this chaotic fashion. Gulf between two languages, two worlds. I tried to imagine in what world Ali lived, how he saw things, and an impression of infinity took hold of me. We would have needed to talk for years, for tens of years ... We should never have met each other and chance had brought us face to face. Chance? Not quite. The strike and its effects, more or less directly. And at the same time I had the feeling that Ali was very close to me. The solitary, obstinate striker, the child with the black dog, Danglois' scapegoat. An obscure brother, emerging for a moment from the darkness which was going to swallow him up again.

In fact he was pushed around from post to post, from one rough joke to another, and the next day he had disappeared. Afterward I received intermittent news of him, through people who knew him by sight ("Oh yes, the tall Moroccan, with the blue tattoo mark on his forehead, the one who hardly ever speaks and still goes out at five o'clock ... Now wait, I think I've seen him carrying tubs around in the paint shop").

Finally I learned that they had settled him at the Javel works.

Cleaning the johns.

7

The work bench

July.

In the soldering shop, where they've just put me back, the heat's stifling. All the metallic surfaces have become hotplates, which surround us and move past us in a burning procession. The ugliness of the metal skeletons nailed together, scorched without their skins. Always the jets of flame from the blowtorches, the showers of white sparks, the burned metal and the hammering of the sheet iron. The car shells, identical and imperturbable, glide through what has become an oven, where we feel we are going to melt and dissolve. Grayness and steam, nothing to breathe except gusts of torrid air, the sickening smell of the burned iron and metal dust. Dirty clothes stick to the sweat, everything becomes clammy and the sweat makes your eyes run.

Gravier's department was short of a laborer to help the man on the hoist who gets the shells up from the yard and deposits them at the start of the line. It'll be me.

The forced labor in the yard lasted nearly four months. Braced behind my carts, my eyes glued to the asphalt, I felt rather than saw the spring go by and the summer begin. Harassed by Danglois, jeered at by Gravier from time to time, I was convinced that they would leave me there until the August shutdown. But they've decided to move me.

So here I am helping the hoist operator, at the entry to the soldering shop. I receive and check the fenders, the hoods, and the doors, and I place them on big iron racks which accompany the shells onto the assembly line. I take defective doors to the retoucher and when they're done I put them back in the circuit. When the shells disappear into the moving tunnel which will take them to the paint shop, the platforms on which they have glided all along the assembly line are automatically thrown out to the edge, where they pile up. It's my job to bring the platforms back regularly to the start of the line, so that the hoist man can put the car shells on them, at the rate of one every three or four minutes.

This hoist man is an Algerian. Kamel. About twenty-five. He has an odd hair-style, like the Beatles, bouffant and covered with brilliantine. At work he wears a greenish boiler suit, with a belt; but outside he's dressed in an aggressive style, blazer with gilt buttons and shoes with pointed toes. Looks like a pimp. In fact they say he is a bit of a pimp. That he's got some odd acquaintances at Pigalle and Barbès, that girls with heavy make-up sometimes come to wait for him at the gate. He's openly arrogant toward me, his "assistant", taking advantage of the situation to give me orders and treat me like a lackey. Apparently, the reason he holds this strategic post, which supplies the assembly line, is that he's shown proof of being really keen, and he sees the rate of production in a way which pleases the bosses. Gravier and Antoine have confidence in him. He has hardly any dealings with the other workers. He reigns over his winch and the entry to the shop, dominating the yard a few feet below with his glance, active, authoritarian, filling up the line without pausing.

One day, during the break, we talked about the strike against recuperation, and he bragged about never having joined it, unlike several "idiots" from 86 who got onto Gravier's bad books. I replied harshly, things hotted up very quickly but our quarrel was interrupted by the line starting up again. Since then we haven't spoken to each other except in the course of working—he making me go faster or shouting at me, and I telling him to go to hell.

Nothing's changed in the soldering shop, since that first day in September 1968—my brief allocation to soldering with tin. Thirty yards away from me Mouloud's carrying out the same movements indefinitely. Tin, torch, back and forth with the little stick, a smooth curve (I know that the impression of facility is only apparent, that you have to control your hand to within one millimeter, contract your muscles and nerves, manage the pressure of your fingers with precision). One 2 CV's done, another appears, curve broken, a crack instead of the soldering: tin, torch, little stick, the curve's smooth again. One 2 CV done, another one to do ... I calculate. One hundred and fifty a day. Two hundred and twenty days a year. At this moment, at the end of July, he must be more or less at his thirty thousandth. Thirty-three thousand times in a year he has made the same movements. While people went to the movies, chatted, made love, swam, skied, picked flowers, played with their children, listened to lectures, stuffed themselves with food, strolled about, talked about the *Critique of Pure Reason*, got together to discuss the barricades, the ghost of civil war, the question of weapons, the working class as a subject and students as a substitute for the subject, and the exemplary action which forces issues into the open and the detonator that sets off the charge, while the sun rose over Granada and the Seine lapped gently under the Pont Alexandre III, while the wind flattened the cornfields, caressed the grass in the meadows and made the leaves rustle in the woods, thirty-three thousand 2 CV car shells have moved by in front of Mouloud since September, so that he can solder thirty-three thousand times the same gap five centimeters long, and each time he's picked up his tin, his torch, his little stick. Upright, gray at the temples, his eyes a little tired, a few extra wrinkles, I think.

The soldering assembly line forms a half-circle. There are thirty or so work positions around it, one after the other, where they carry out the hundred or so soldering jobs which the car shell must have before leaving shop number 86.

One work position apart from the others. There,

separately within the arc of the circle, an elderly worker, alone in front of his bench, retouches the unsatisfactory doors. On his left a heap of damaged doors which I pile up after a rapid check of those arriving at the start of the line. Cracks, bumps, parts which have been nailed or molded irregularly, lumps and holes, they're for him. He re-does everything, repairs everything, and piles up on his right the doors which have become normal again. I come to take them from there and put them back into the circuit with their car bodies, near the end of the semicircle, in front of the buffer which will send the whole thing to the paint shop.

This door retoucher is a Frenchman. A man with white hair, meticulous, whose skillful gestures I watch with admiration. You would think him a little artisan, and he appears almost out of place, forgotten like a remnant of another era in the repeated interlinked movement of the workshop. He has many tools at his disposal—instruments for punching, hammering, and polishing, soldering irons, tin, blowtorches, all mingled in a kind of familiar bric-à-brac where he finds everything without hesitation—and each retouching embodies a particular operation, hardly ever identical to the preceding one. It is the chance occurrences in the pressing work, in transport, with jolts and collisions, parts which fall onto the floor or are struck by some fork lift, which determine what he will have to repair, stop, solder, polish, rectify. Each time, he picks up the defective door, looks at it carefully, passes a finger over the irregularities (he examines as attentively as a surgeon before an operation), puts it down, makes his decision, arranges the tools he'll need, and gets to work. He works bending down, at ten or twenty centimeters from the metal, precise with the stroke of his file or his hammer, only drawing back to avoid the shower of sparks from soldering or the metal chips from sanding. A craftsman, almost an artist.

The most amazing thing is his bench.

An indefinable object, made out of scraps of metal and rods, all kinds of odd supports, improvised vices to hold the parts, with holes everywhere and a disturbing air of instability. It's only a semblance. Never has the work bench betrayed him or collapsed. And, when you watch him working for a fairly long time, you realize that all the apparent imperfections of the bench have their uses: through that crack he can slide an instrument which will hold a concealed part in position; through that hole he will pass the rod for a difficult soldering job; through this empty space underneath—which makes the whole thing look so fragile—he will be able to finish some hammering work without having to turn over the door which is already held in position. He had put together this do-it-yourself work bench, modified, transformed, and completed it. Now he's part and parcel of it, he knows its resources by heart: two turns of a screw here, three turns of a nut there, a strut raised by two notches, a slope rectified by a few degrees, and the door is exactly as it should be so that he can solder, polish, file, and hammer at the exact spot of the retouching, however off-center and difficult it may be to reach—above, below, from the side, at angles, at a slant, at the interior of a curve, at the edge of a rim.

This retoucher is called Demarcy. He has several qualifications, in metalwork and soldering. He's a craftsman—P1, I think, or something like that. In the soldering shop he's the only craftsman working on production. (In the other shops there are a few craftsmen on production, usually on machines. But the majority of the craftsmen at the plant are on tooling work or maintenance.)

His age, his qualifications, his experience all mean that he enjoys a certain respect. Nobody says *tu* to him, people avoid playing jokes on him. Even the foreman and the section manager modify their usual tones of voice when they speak to him. Almost courtesy.

Demarcy doesn't regard himself as an important man. When he speaks to someone he always does so politely. It's true that this happens rarely. He concentrates deeply on his work and gives the impression of being a man of somewhat taciturn character, while the relative isolation of the post seems to suit him. He does what he has to do, he asks nothing of anyone and no one asks anything of him. As a rule, if he has a problem—an instrument that breaks, or a substance which happens to be lacking—he resolves it himself: he repairs the tool or goes off to get one from the store, or fiddles about with his work bench in order to invent a new method.

Now, in this second fortnight of July a threat hangs over Demarcy and his work bench. The retoucher is under consideration in the work-study office—but he doesn't know it yet.

In this second fortnight of July, when the torpor of summer already overwhelms us, when smells of sweat mingle together ever more strongly, when the workshops are transformed into furnaces, when men faint more often than usual in the paint shop, and women in upholstery as well, when the air becomes thick, when liquids stagnate more quickly, when weights weigh heavier, when tongues become dry and clothing damp, when at every break we crowd toward the openings in search of hypothetical fresh air, during this second fortnight of July, work-study is on the prowl.

The senior staff is overtaken with a slight attack of fever. They're not to be seen any more.

There are changes, transfers, regroupings.

Modifications are made in production.

New cars have just been introduced into our 2 CV assembly lines. Ami 8s. For every four or five 2 CVs there is one Ami 8. At the same time some posts have been modified, new tools have been added or old tools changed.

Rationalization, as they say.

They're timing (discreetly: the white coat walks about with the chronometer in his pocket, stands behind the fellow who's working, a click in his pocket, the man makes his usual movements, a click at the end of the operation, nothing seen or heard; he only has to move away at a walking pace and read the result quietly, some way off; it's noted). All that's put on record, you're taken apart and put together again to the tenth of a second and, one fine day, they come to make a surprise change in your piece-work. "Well, yes, they've done the calculations again up there, old man. Here are the new times."—"But ..."—(weary gesture from the white coat, hypocritical) "It's nothing to do with me," and he goes off quickly.

Rationalization.

Why now? It's the good moment, they don't do anything by chance. They have sociologists, psychologists, studies, statistics, specialists in human relations, people who do human sciences, they have informers, interpreters, yellow trade unionists, they have the senior staff testing the ground, and they compare the experiment at Choisy with the one at Javel, and the one at Levallois, and the one at Clichy, and they ask the opinion of the other bosses, and they hold conferences, and they distribute credits in order to get to know all this better, and then study the conflicts, and the conduct of the immigrant workers, and the mentality of the average semiskilled worker, and absenteeism, and so on and so on.

In two weeks, holidays. They know it's too late for a strike to break out. They know above all that the immigrants have only one thing in their heads now: they have to manage to spend their holidays in their own countries. Find the money, find the ticket that's not too expensive, the special plane, the boat, the third class, the all-in trip on deck, or the short flight from Marseilles to Oran for a hundred and fifty people. There's chaos in travel agencies, sailing companies, airline reservations. The plant is overwhelmed with travel fever. During the breaks, in the canteen, it's the stock exchange: a return ticket to Batna at so much, Paris-Algiers at a cheaper rate, a group travel ticket from Marseilles to Algiers, but there must be ten people travelling together. And for Yugoslavia there's a golden opportunity, but you must leave on July 27th, three days before the factory shuts. Those who know they won't be able to leave, because they're broke, or haven't anyone to see at home, wander about like dead souls, indifferent to everything, heartbroken by this agitation which leads to their involuntary exclusion. Those who will try to get away think only of that. Their thoughts are already there: in the Kabylian or Croatian village, in the suburbs of Algiers or Barcelona, in the little farms of Tras Os Montes or the olive groves of Alentejo. Their thoughts are already among the fishermen and the wine growers, among the flocks of sheep or in the shoemakers' stalls, in the village square at the time for talk and gossip, when the sun sets gently behind the hills. Their thoughts are with their parents, wife, children, brothers, sisters, uncles, aunts, cousins, friends. Out there. There's only the body here at Citroën's disposal. But the body's enough for Citroën. All the better in fact, if the thoughts have gone, they'll take advantage of the fact. They'll get a little more from the body, now's the time.

Rationalization.

All that Citroën will have succeeded in grinding out of them, from the productivity point of view, during this second fortnight of July, will be so much gained for the reopening at the end of August or early in September. From the first day of the new session "normal production" will be, certainly, the highest norms registered at the end of July.

Another reason. In a year from now, two years at the most, Choisy will finally close its gates. It's official. Citroën's selling the land, demolishing the buildings. There will be tower apartment blocks: a splendid piece of property development, with the price of a square yard of ground in Paris as it is! The equipment will be taken out and production will be divided up between other plants, more modern ones, especially in the outer suburbs, where land is less expensive. The work force will be split up and transferred more or less everywhere. Those who don't like their new allocation can leave (and one can count on the management to take care of all the troublemakers, trade unionists, and hotheads: there's no shortage of isolated jobs at the other end of France!).

Before the big move, you might as well do the housework: reduce times, pare down the number of jobs, dishonestly win an extra operation here, another one there, find a job for a left-hander who remained shockingly idle during work for right-handers, change an out-of-date machine, replace a gimlet with a more rapid one, two tools by one which can be used for two jobs. Etc.

So work-study is on the prowl.

It doesn't really have a name, work-study.

It has one in principle: "the time and motion study department." "Time and motion," say the initiated. But it's remote and anonymous, unknown to many. You don't even know where it is, you don't know the people. So, when there's something new you simply say "they": "Have you seen what they've just given me to do extra? They're not idle, up there ..." There are circulars which arrive in the foreman's office, staff notices, urgent decisions (but he doesn't show them to everyone, certainly, only to the charge hand with whom he has discussions in a low voice within the secrecy of his glass-walled cage). There are unknown white coats who come walking around, watching us work (no doubt with stopwatches in their pockets: click, click, in secret ...), then they go off to write in their notebooks in a corner of the workshop. Others come to inspect the tools. And I look at your blowtorch, I finger your gimlet, no "Good morning" or "Good afternoon", I haven't seen you, I make notes in my little book and I go to see the next man.

There are machines they change unexpectedly, without warning. Oh, they've brought another blowtorch, with a spring so that it can go back into place on its own. (Don't worry, my friend, they've timed the spring up there: less five seconds, the time you needed to put the blowtorch back in its place. They're getting ready to reduce your time or to lumber you with an extra operation. In any case, those five seconds won't be wasted!)

And then one car more here, one car more there.

And then the time clocks are advanced slightly. They show seven o'clock when everyone's watches show seven minutes to seven. And the lines start up on the dot.

Supposed to be seven o'clock. In fact, two minutes to seven. Two minutes stolen doesn't seem much, but it means half a 2 CV free of charge every day, without anyone realizing it. Every two days a finished car manufactured outside the official working time, between two minutes to seven and seven o'clock. Not bad, is it?

It's on the prowl, work-study. Usually anonymous, present only in its results. But sometimes it acquires a face, a punctually concrete form, and here it is going on to attack in person, at a point on the front where it wasn't expected. By Demarcy, for example. Why Demarcy? Try to find an answer! Never any hold-up in his job, the retouched doors are perfect. So?

You can have hypotheses about it. For example, a white coat wandering around on inspection may have winced at the sight of this do-it-yourself, unorthodox work bench. What's that thing? And, in fact, if you watch Demarcy work for just two or three minutes, he seems to waste time tinkering with his bench, moving nuts about, adjusting the wedges. Obviously, if you watch for a long time you realize that all this is in order and that the retoucher uses his bench to excellent advantage. But the fellows from work-study won't spend hours at each work position: a few glances and they're certain they've understood. They've followed courses and everything, they know about the scientific organization of work! Yes, a guy from time and motion may well have passed this way and told himself that this over-fragile bench caused a loss of time: I note in my book "Post R 82, workshop 86, replace work bench, install a model F 675 with adjustable pitch," I close my notebook, I adjust my spectacles, and I go off to stick my nose in somewhere else, I have to take back to the office my quota of seconds to be stolen and machines to be "improved".

Another hypothesis. Suppose that they'll want to duplicate Demarcy's post in the future organization of work, after the assembly lines have been moved out of Choisy. For example, they might go up to four hundred cars a day. And for retouching the doors in the soldering shop they'd put two men, side by side, who would do exactly the same thing (or one would do the front doors and the other the back doors, like that they'd be a little more specialized). Note that in duplicating on this basis they'd make a nice gain in productivity (twice one hundred and fifty cars, that only makes three hundred: the move, the more modern machines, the specialization, would allow them to give the two men a hundred more). Fine, this must be prepared. And in the first place this incredible do-it-yourself work bench must be replaced by a "normal" bench, which can be reproduced exactly in two copies for the post that has been duplicated, maybe three or four copies, if one sees things in a big way. No more little old craftsman! Four, five, six Demarcys at work benches that have been made normal, making exactly the same movements, with retouching that's been costed, classified, normalized, and shared out by a superintendent! No more improvisation, precision to within one second. Easy for piece-work arrangements, effective for large-scale production. And suppose that they want to go beyond the norm to working in teams, eight threes. The work bench would no longer be used by one single worker, but by three in succession. No more room for individualism, for the little machine put together for one man. We need an all-purpose thing, strong and simple, even if a little less practical. Above all a machine that isn't personalized. Normalized.

Or else there's been a special study on retouching, covering all the Citroën places, with plenty of graphs, statistics, and curves, and it's been decided that one could reduce the costs of production by minimizing spoiled parts, calculating the times more precisely, modernizing the equipment. Conferences, meetings, inspections, staff notes, the plan is adopted. And, at the right moment, the second fortnight in July, when the specialists from the "social" department and the personnel services confirm that they can go ahead, that it's the moment to push up working speeds and try out something new, bang, it falls on Demarcy, the door retoucher working quietly in the soldering shop.

To be precise, on Demarcy's work bench.

Without warning, one morning, at precisely a quarter past eight.

Tuesday, July 22nd, eight fifteen (they take advantage of the break in order not to disturb the operation of the workshop), the decks are cleared for combat in number 86. Three men arrive with a huge winch, hoist an object of solid cast iron up to the level of the shop, let it run along the line which has been cleared in advance of cars in the course of manufacture, and finally bring it, not without difficulty, to Demarcy's place. His old bench is promptly cleared, thrown into a rubbish corner of the shop, among old cloths and rusty drums, and this one's installed for him instead. The three fellows wipe their faces vigorously, go get a paper signed by Gravier, and disappear.

Work starts again.

Demarcy looks with astonishment at this work bench which has fallen from the sky. Or rather from the unforeseeable caprices of the time and motion department. A huge, solid cube, topped with an inclined plane, on which to place the door. Two bolts at the sides, in order to fix it. That's all. The sloping surface is plain, all in metal. There are no more of those holes and passages which allowed Demarcy to work above, below, at the edge, without changing the position of the door.

He touches the object. Examines the possibilities of adjusting it. Limited. Walks round it. Touches it with his fingertips. Scratches his head, puffing, slightly breathless. (Passing near him, I hear him murmur: "Oh, just fancy that!") Nostalgic glance at his old bench, thrown away at the back of the shop, which will rust away there before going off to the scrap heap. Demarcy looks upset. He's not the type to complain and protest. He remains there, his arms dangling, absorbing the shock, he repeats: "Oh, just fancy ... that!" The racket has started again in the workshop, everyone is concentrating on what he has to do, on the car shell that's gliding slowly in front of his position, and no one now has time to pay attention to Demarcy. Alone with his confusion, without appeal.

The line's operating again and the heap of defective doors is growing, while that of retouched doors is going down dangerously. Demarcy will certainly have to try to catch up. With the clumsy movements of a beginner, he starts. He wedges a first door, instinctively looks for means of access which are now closed, decides to separate the operations which he used to carry out simultaneously, using both hands, above and below. He begins to file.

One door, with difficulty. Another.

No doubt about it, it's a catastrophe.

Demarcy's rhythm is broken, his method of working gone to pieces. Every time he has to work on a door from underneath he's obliged to unscrew the nuts from the vices, turn the door over, and tighten the screws again. No means of proceeding, as he was accustomed to doing, by rapid over-under combined movements, the easiest way of re-establishing a smooth surface with hammering. Before he used to use his left hand to wedge a piece under the door, gradually moving it along, and with his right hand, he would give precise little hammerstrokes, progressively straightening out the metal area by area. Impossible, now: he has to work the right side and then the reverse side separately: and waste his time unscrewing, turning over, screwing up again ... With this new work bench he needs at least half again the time with each door.

About ten in the morning Gravier comes along to have a look. Not necessary to do a drawing for him. On seeing the old man struggling, he understands at once the stupidity of the exchange. He looks heavenward, shrugs his shoulders; his mimicry shows clearly what he's thinking: "Don't know what to invent any more, those bureaucrats from time and motion. Would do better to ask our opinion about production, we know the job. Well, it's their business ..." It doesn't depend on him and, obviously, the time and motion people haven't even consulted him. No question of him making a criticism in front of a worker. The hierarchy is the hierarchy. The foreman goes away without saying anything. Demarcy must sort himself out. If there's a break in the supply of retouched doors they'll notice it. No doubt then there'll have to be a report to the time and motion people. For the moment that's not the case. Demarcy works three times as hard as before, he's getting nervous and irritable, but on the whole he keeps up—with less advance, it's true, but that's his problem. The essential thing for the foreman is for the assembly line to be supplied. Otherwise ... "The representative of the management is not an office for weeping in," he's fond of saying.

For Demarcy the worst is yet to come.

Canteen. (The old man stays in the workshop; he carefully sets up his dish of beef stew and boiled potatoes, gets out his bread and beer, and eats silently on an empty barrel near his bench, chewing each mouthful slowly.)

Work starts again.

Three o'clock in the afternoon. The shop's been heating up fiercely since we started again at one o'clock. Heat of metal and sweat. We feel overwhelmed. Difficult to breathe. Every time I go by Demarcy, or when I come to supply him with faulty parts and take away those he's retouched, I watch him work for a moment. It's not going well. I've seen him struggling with the huge cast iron object, trying out different methods, changing the order of the operations ... in vain. He has in fact lost a third of his effectiveness. He's only just afloat: if he fails with one or two doors, if he gives a few hammerstrokes the wrong way, if there are any mishaps with a blowtorch he'll get behind.

Three fifteen. Break for a snack. Everyone collapses. It must be at least thirty degrees. Too stifling to talk. Air!

Three twenty-five. The line starts again with a groan, with a clicking of hooks, the squeak of its gears—all these machines which vibrate beneath our feet—the crash of the first car shell which Kamel throws into the circuit ("O.K., get on with it," the charge hand has just shouted to the hoist man, and the hoist man starts off at high speed, *he* doesn't have to be asked). We drag ourselves out of our somnolence, take our tools. Showers of sparks. Flames from the blowtorches. Hammerstrokes. Punchstrokes. Scraping of the files.

Iron, cast iron, metal, sheet metal, walls and ceiling, fabrics, skins, everything is hot, everything is burning, vapors and sweats, oils and greases.

Half-past three. What's this, now? The workshop's invaded. White coats, blue coats, adjustors' overalls, three-piece suits with ties ... They walk with a firm step, along a five-yard front, talk loudly, pushing aside anything that's in their way. No doubt about it, they're on their own ground, all this belongs to them, they're the masters. Surprise visit from the landlords, the proprietors, however you like to put it (of course, legally, they're salaried staff, like everyone else. But look at them: the top-drawer salaried staff, they're already directors, and as they go by they crush you with a look as though you were an insect). Smart, the suits, with narrow stripes, creases wherever they should be, perfect, pressed (what an oaf you feel, suddenly, in your stained tunic, full of holes, soaked with sweat and oil from lugging unclad sheet metal about), just their ties slightly loose in some cases, because of the heat, and a complete sample of horrible executive faces, the pudgy faces of the old senior men, the bespectacled faces of the young engineers, freshly emerged from the *grande école*, and those who're trying to have the energetic look of the executive who wants something, the one who smokes Marlboros, sprays himself with exotic aftershave and can make a decision in two seconds (*he* must be a yachtsman), and the servile features of the one who trots along just behind the most senior director in the group, the ambitious man with the attaché case, determined never to move more than two feet from his senior, and well-combed hair, regular partings, fashionable hair-styles, brilliantine by the pound, cheeks closely shaved in comfortable bathrooms, ironed coats without a mark on them, bureaucrats' paunches, note pads, briefcases, files ... How many are they? Seven or eight, but they make enough noise for fifteen, talk loudly, circle around in the workshop. The foreman Gravier has bounded out of his glass-walled cage to greet them ("Good morning, sir ... blablabla ... Yes, Sir ... as the assistant departmental chief said ... told ... the figures ... here ... the list ... since this morning ... blablabla ... Sir") and Antoine the charge hand also rushes along to stick himself into the troop, and even Danglois, the adjustor from the yellow union, appearing from God knows where, brings his gray coat and his pile of fat to accompany these gentlemen. And all these fine people come, go, look, take notice, push by you, send someone to look for this, someone to look for that.

In the middle, their chief. The director of something or other (but very high up in the Citroën hierarchy, close collaborator of Bercot, if you please). Bineau. Plump, with an authoritarian air, trussed up in a dark three-piece suit, with a rosette in his buttonhole. He looks like the kind of man who reads *Le Figaro* at the back of a gleaming black DS while the chauffeur, who wears a cap, performs a slalom through the traffic jams. Bineau leads the dance. He doesn't look easy, that one: it wouldn't be worth your while trying to tell him any made-up stories. Piercing gaze, rasping voice, be precise, be brief, I understand quickly, my time's worth a lot of money, much much more than you'll see in a whole year. A real leader of men. Better: a manager. His eye fixed on the irregular curve of the cashflow.

Now, they've snorted for a few minutes, poked their noses into practically every thing in the shop. Bineau gets them together again. They stand in a circle, listen. Then, in a splendid movement all together they go toward Demarcy. On top of Demarcy, I should say, they stick so close together and get so close to him, leaving him hardly the minimum space for his movements.

So there are the ten or so big bugs, standing around in a circle watching the old man work. Bineau gives a few more words of explanation (I'm some way off, with Kamel, but I hear odd scraps: "... example of modernization of the equipment ... adjustment system ... to normalize the posts outside the line ... work-study ... to generalize ... pilot operation ... look at the targets again ... gear down later ... concentrate ... make cuts ... tooling budget ... results ... over six months ..."). From time to time he points out

Demarcy in the process of working. I feel then I'm present at a hospital demonstration, with the professor, the house doctors, the nurses, where the old man would represent the corpse—or at a guided visit to the zoo, with Demarcy as a monkey. He also shows the brand-new work bench or a defective door (which he grabs hold of unceremoniously under the retoucher's nose). The briefing comes to an end, but they all stay there, watching the old man at work.

They've enlarged the circle a little—they were so crowded that the heat was beginning to make them uncomfortable)—they loosen their ties a little, one knot more, they take up more relaxed poses and supports—paunches forward, arms folded, hands clasped over their briefcases—and they follow attentively the retoucher's movements, observing his hands, observing his new bench, observing his tools. Sometimes, Bineau examines the hammer that Demarcy has just put down, or else the blowtorch, or perhaps a door—without ever saying a word to him. Besides, what could he say to him? Something like: "Go on, my friend, go on just as though we weren't here?" What would be the point? In any case, Bineau doesn't seem to have the paternalistic touch, there's no question of wasting his breath.

The spectacle could have gone on like this without any hitch until the end of the day.

Unfortunately Demarcy's beginning to lose his grip.

For him the day is certainly without mercy. Starting in the morning, with the arrival of the cast iron object and the disappearance of his old bench. Years of habit, repeated movements he knows by heart, years of experience, scrapped in one move. Fine, he's tried to confront and surmount the obstacle, by concentrating, by holding on, by trying to invent with each movement—against this great brute of a machine produced straight from the head of a bureaucrat who's never held a hammer or a file. But he needed all his attention. And how to keep it up with this troop of bosses crowding around to disturb him, to throw him off balance and upset him? He tries to keep his head bent over his work bench but can't prevent himself from glancing up from below, and jumping each time he hears Bineau's loud voice. His hands are less sure. He no longer knows in what order he should carry out his operations. Wasn't there a list of jobs, up there, of which he's long since forgotten the wording? What he used to do by instinct he's now trying to do in accordance with instructions, and in the way it should be done in relation to this accursed object. He gets into a muddle. Starts hammering without having wedged the two sides—the door slips, he catches hold of it again, does some soldering, does some more (the hand that holds the soldering iron trembles), for the third soldering job he has to turn the door over, he unscrews, hammers, blushes, embarrassed because he realizes he's just made an unnecessary operation, which cannot have escaped his formidable audience: he should have finished one side, soldering and hammering, before turning over the door and wedging it again, but he's let himself be carried away by the old habits connected with the former bench, when he was free to go above and below when he wanted, doing all the soldering first, then the hammering, then the sanding ...

Murmurs from the circle of senior people.

Bineau wrinkles his brows.

Demarcy, crimson and sweating, tries not to see them, to work on top of his retouching in order to keep up appearances, he bends further over, tries to go faster, but the huge cast iron object frustrates his attempts, crushes his margin of maneuvering. Once more the unnecessary operations, the same door turned over three or four times (and, each time: unscrew, wedge, screw up again), soldering that lacks precision, retouching that's less clean ... Demarcy's white hair clings to his forehead, matted together, he's snorting like a bull, drops of sweat run down his neck and make the blue collar of his tunic wet ...

Metallic ring. Through an oversharp gesture he's dropped his hammer on the floor. Bends down quickly to pick ...

"For goodness' sake! What's all this muddle?"

Bineau's voice, loud and angry, has cut short the old man's movement. For a second he remains bent, frozen in his posture, his fingers a few inches away from the hammer. Then he continues his movement slowly and comes up again shamefaced, while the director explodes and sputters.

Bineau: "I've been watching you for a quarter of an hour. You're doing just anything! The best machines are no good if the man using them doesn't make an effort to understand their functioning and use them correctly. You're given a modern system, carefully perfected, and that's what you do with it!"

Demarcy: "I don't know what's come over me, sir ... Perhaps it's tiredness ... Usually ..."

Gravier: "Listen, old man, don't tell Monsieur Bineau your life story. You'd better listen to what he has to tell you and try to work correctly."

The briefcase carrier with spectacles and brilliantined hair who's standing just behind Bineau, half-aloud but loud enough for the old man to hear him: "You wonder sometimes how they get their CAP."*

Farther back, a whole buzz of scandalized, unpleasant, and insulting remarks.

The old man lowers his head and says nothing.

What a filthy trick. Gravier knows very well that the new work bench is no good. He knows very well that it's not the old man's fault. Antoine, the charge hand, knows it too. The whole soldering shop knows Demarcy very well, his precision, his experience. But nobody will say so. Nobody will say anything. The work-study office is always right. And you don't argue with a director at Bineau's level.

The old man had to swallow his humiliation to the very end. To the last minute of his working day. Leaning, clumsy and unsure, over work which had become suddenly strange and formidable. With all that gang around him, as though they were putting a young man through a

---

* Certificate of professional aptitude.

professional exam, nudging each other with their elbows, putting on shocked expressions, making remarks. And Gravier pretending to teach him his job ("But no, Demarcy, begin with the soldering!"), him, the old craftsman who's never messed up a part for years and whose skill had been, until now, respected by everyone.

A few days later the three strong men came again for the new work bench and put the old man's former one back in place. Gravier must have negotiated this on the quiet with the time and motion department. Rationalization would certainly return to the attack on another occasion, there was plenty of time.

This new substitution was made without any fuss, and nobody thought it wise to say a word to Demarcy about the "incident". Moreover, at no moment throughout the whole business had anyone pretended to consult him.

The old man went back to his retouching on his old bench, apparently as in the past. But now there was a kind of terror in his eyes which I had not noticed in him before. He seemed to feel he was being spied on. Temporary reprieve. As though he was waiting for the next blow. He became even more inward-looking, always anxious when anyone spoke a word to him. Sometimes he would spoil a door, a thing which had hardly ever happened to him "before".

Soon afterwards, he fell ill.

Intensification of speeds.
Times unexpectedly reduced.
Piece-work payments modified.
Machines totally changed.
One job abolished.
Rationalization.

The Bineau gang must have caused damage in other places, apart from the soldering shop. They're furious in the paint shop. Mohamed, the Kabylian shepherd, who's a paint sprayer, came to see me. We must resist. We must get the committee going again. Draw up leaflets. Describe what has happened. Prepare an action. Not straightaway: a few days before the holidays it wouldn't be any good, you can't make the works move now. But as soon as it reopens. From the first week of September. I agree, Mohamed. As soon as September comes we'll get it going again. Giving out leaflets, meetings in the basement, the hard work of agitation during the breaks, in the cloakrooms, in the canteen, in the café, in the hostels. Leaflets in all languages, put up in the johns, circulating around the assembly lines, passed from hand to hand, spelled out in low voices for those who can't read. Against the intensification of work and the whims of the time and motion department. And also against the arbitrary transfers when Choisy closes. Let workers have equivalent jobs in the other plants in the Paris area. Jojo, the old craftsman in the paint shop, says that the CGT's going to launch a campaign of the same kind.

I begin at once—and Mohamed too, on his side. Again I go around all the people I know to talk to them about it. The Tunisian with the pockmarked face in the soldering shop. Sadok. Mouloud. A Spaniard. A Malian laborer—a new one, with whom I've had a few discussions. People from the upholstery shop, whom I see again from time to time. Simon. Go through it with Mohamed, at the Café des Sports. Yes, a counterattack is possible, immediately after the interruption of the holidays. The surface appears to be calm, but deep down a new wave's forming, which will swell and hurl itself against them.

Wednesday, July 30, 1969. End of the afternoon. Only a few more minutes' work and we stop for a month.

I'm called to the central office.

Pass. Underground corridor. Administrative buildings, on the other side of the Avenue de Choisy. Office. Papers.

I'm dismissed with notice (I do not have to work out the period of notice).

"Reduction of staff."

I refuse to sign the "all accounts settled" ("As you wish,

it's not important"), seize the envelope, run to see Klatzman, the CGT delegate (he works on this side of the boulevard, on tool-making, a remote post where the management sent him so that he couldn't do anything outside the hours set aside for delegates' work: in urgent cases you have to go see him there). Klatzman reads all the papers, asks me to explain a few details. There's nothing to be done on the legal side. Citroën has complied with the rules. As for attempting some action, such as a leaflet ...; the plant's in the process of closing down for a month!

Klatzman's right. They've played it well. Nothing to be done. I'd have preferred a more epic dismissal.

But the wave's gathering deep down, it will rise anyway. And, after that one, there'll be others.

I thank Klatzman, we'll meet again. I go off to say goodbye to my mates in the shop. Too late. The plant's already been closed for a few minutes, everyone's rushed to the exit, the cloakrooms emptied in half a moment. A month far away. Quick, quick.

The plant's closed.

The yard's empty, clear. No more car shells, finished cars, fork lifts, containers, trailers. An ordinary yard. A few dozen square yards of asphalt, its gray lighter than usual in the July sunshine. The door's still half-open. The guard's unfastened his jacket, taken off his cap, he's scratching his head. Behind him a fellow walks diagonally across the yard, his hands in his pockets, without hurrying. An impression of rest.

Barely a quarter of an hour ago the production of 2 CVs was going ahead at full tilt, twelve hundred people were working hard in the noise and the burning heat.

Now, silence. The last workers are going off, turning the corner of the boulevard.

Nobody any more.

I look at the plant.

Seen from the street it looks inoffensive, with its gray, medium-sized buildings merging into the landscape.

Girls go by in light-colored dresses. The sun's really hot.
The colors, the holidays.

I light a cigarette.
I go toward the Café des Sports, slowly.

Oh, there's Kamel. The man from the hoist, in his city
clothes. Still looks just as much the pimp. Blazer, flared
trousers, incredible multi-colored tie. He dawdles as he sees
me coming. You might think he was waiting for me. What
does Kamel want?

I don't particularly want to talk to him. There are so
many others I'd like to see again just now, and it's got to be
Kamel who's waiting for me! This evening I'm going to see
Mohamed at his hostel, to tell him about my dismissal. I
won't go to see Simon until the holidays are over. His wife's
better, they're going on vacation for the first time in years.
To his parents-in-law, near Melun ("The country", he
talks about it as though it was in Amazonia!). For a week
he's been unable to keep still out of impatience: today I
prefer to leave him in peace. Sadok I'll go and see this
evening, I know where to find him. The other workmates
are in the wilds. Some are frantically locking their suitcases
or already crowding into busses or trains. The others are
scattered throughout the districts to the north of Paris,
forgetting, for one evening at least, that they're not going
away.

No friend I can confide in. I would so much like to talk to
Primo, Georges, Christian, Mouloud, Ali, Sadok, Simon,
Jojo. Nobody. I'll have to wait.

Just Kamel, there outside the Café des Sports, right in
the sun. Fashion-plate. Kamel the overkeen, who spent his
time pushing me, acting the boss, pushing up the speed.
Kamel to whom I've nothing to say.

He, on the other hand, seems to want to start a
conversation.

A few steps more. I've gotten to where he is. What does
he want?

I say to him, drily:

"I've been fired."

He: "I know, someone told me ..."

Silence.

Kamel, again: "Listen ..."

He stops, changes his stance as though he had pins and needles in his legs. Rustle of the flared polyester trousers. He irritates me, twisting about like that. He goes on.

Kamel: "Listen, they offered me money to start a row with you, they wanted to get rid of you that way."

I: "Well?"

Kamel: "Well, I refused."

I: "Why?"

Kamel: "Because ... because I don't need money. Not that money."

He's got no trace of his arrogance, he looks embarrassed—about what? That they'd thought of him for this dirty work? Suddenly he says goodbye and disappears around the corner of the street. I'm sure he was telling the truth. I even suspect that it was Danglois who asked him.

I think: Kamel, too, he's working-class.

The people, events, objects, and locations of this story are true. I have only changed the names of a few people.